TELL YOU SOON

BOOKS BY JAN THOMPSON

CITY/COASTAL/BEACH ROMANCE

Seaside Chapel (7 Books)

JanThompson.com/seaside

Savannah Sweethearts (12 Books)

JanThompson.com/savannah

Vacation Sweethearts (8 Books)

JanThompson.com/vacation

ROMANTIC SUSPENSE/THRILLERS

Protector Sweethearts (6 Books)

JanThompson.com/protector

Defender Sweethearts (6 Books)

JanThompson.com/defender

Binary Hackers (4 Books)

JanThompson.com/binary

JanThompson.com/books

TELL YOU SOON

SAVANNAH SWEETHEARTS
BOOK THREE

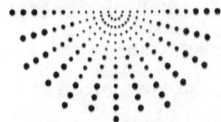

JAN THOMPSON

GEORGIA
PRESS

TELL YOU SOON (SAVANNAH SWEETHEARTS BOOK 3)

Copyright © 2015 Jan Edttii Lim Thompson

Book News: JanThompson.com/newsletter
Author Website: JanThompson.com
Published by Georgia Press LLC

This book is a work of fiction. All characters, persons, places, events, and things either are the product of the author's active imagination or are used fictitiously.

Scripture taken from the New King James Version®. Copyright © 1982 by Thomas Nelson. Used by permission. All rights reserved.

The Belford's Savannah Seafood & Steaks restaurant, in which Ming and Sabine dined, is mentioned with permission from its proprietor.

eBook Cover Design: Georgia Press LLC
Paperback Cover Design: Georgia Press and Deranged Doctor Design

eBook ISBN 978-1-944188-02-3
Paperback ISBN 978-1-944188-27-6

To my Lord and Savior, Jesus Christ, who died on the cross to save me from my sins and rose again from the grave to give me eternal life in heaven.

For God so loved the world that He gave His only begotten Son, that whoever believes in Him should not perish but have everlasting life.
—John 3:16

READ A FREE EBOOK IN THE SAME STORY WORLD

Set in Georgia, South Carolina, and Tennessee, this clean and wholesome Christian romance tells the story of art gallery archivist Sheryl Breckenridge and world-famous sculptor Winton Pace. Read this ebook for free!

Time for Me (A Vacation Sweethearts Prequel)
JanThompson.com/time-free

ABOUT THE SAVANNAH SWEETHEARTS SERIES

From *USA Today* bestselling author Jan Thompson come these clean and wholesome Christian romances set on the romantic beaches of Tybee Island and in the coastal city of Savannah, Georgia, two of the most romantic coastal towns in the world.

Against a backdrop of ocean, sand, and sun, these inspirational stories showcase aspects of the human need for God and for one another. Have some tea, settle in a comfortable reading chair, and enjoy these celebrations of faith, hope, and love in Jesus Christ.

SAVANNAH SWEETHEARTS

- Book 1: Ask You Later
- Book 2: Know You More

- Book 3: Tell You Soon
- Book 4: Draw You Near
- Book 5: Cherish You So
- Book 6: Walk You There
- Book 7: Love You Always
- Book 8: Kiss You Now
- Book 9: Find You Again
- Book 10: Wish You Joy
- Book 11: Call You Home
- Book 12: Let You Go

While Savannah Sweethearts books can be read as standalone stories, you can see a bigger picture of the Riverside Chapel community and get a glimpse of the futures of previous characters if you read Books 1-12 in order.

Savannah Sweethearts:
JanThompson.com/sweethearts

For book news, sign up for Jan's mailing list:
JanThompson.com/newsletter

YOU ARE READING TELL YOU SOON

SAVANNAH SWEETHEARTS BOOK 3

She wants to fix up his beach house and move on.
He wants to fix up her heart and move in.

A private investigator trying to sell his house falls in love with his colleague's sister and gets her into mortal danger.

A Christian beach romance with suspense, *Tell You Soon* is Book 3 in *USA Today* bestselling author Jan Thompson's Savannah Sweethearts series of clean and wholesome, sweet and inspirational, contemporary Christian romances set in the coastal city of Savannah, Georgia, and on the beaches of Tybee Island by the Atlantic Ocean.

SABINE'S SCARS...

Sabine Hu's legs were crushed in an auto accident three years ago, ending her modeling career. Today she walks without a cane, is back in heels, and has found a new job as a real estate agent selling houses in Savannah and on Tybee Island.

She keeps to herself and stays in the background, unlike her high-profile sister, Helen, whose fame as a private investigator is constantly in the news.

MING'S MAYHEM...

Private Investigator Aidan Ming Wei works with Sabine's sister, but he's interested in getting to know Sabine better. He thinks he can draw her out of her shell. Since he has hired Sabine to sell his house by the Atlantic Ocean, he has all sorts of excuses to spend time with her.

She seems to be at ease around him, and they get along well.

However, spending time with her is exactly what would put her life in danger, and Ming risks losing Sabine forever...

Tell You Soon (Savannah Sweethearts Book 3):
JanThompson.com/tell

Savannah Sweethearts:
JanThompson.com/sweethearts

For book news, sign up for Jan's mailing list:
JanThompson.com/newsletter

TELL YOU SOON

CHAPTER ONE

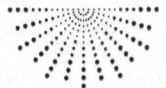

*a*idan Ming Wei couldn't remember how he had been somehow drafted into planning the wedding for his sister, Heidi, to Pastor Diego Flores of Riverside Chapel.

He vaguely remembered that Heidi's best friends had been trying to cut down the costs of hosting a riverboat wedding cruise, and the best way to do that—according to them!—was to avoid hiring a professional wedding planner. The bridesmaids—Abilene, Nadine, and Piper—had divvied up the work among the friends, and somehow Ming had drawn the shortest straw.

They had assigned him to be in charge of invitations.

Invitations!

He remembered telling them: *I'll just send everyone an email.*

And he had done that, much to his friends' chagrin.

Everything had gone well, from the wedding to the reception. After taking the newlyweds to the airport for their three-week honeymoon in Italy, Ming had jumped right back into work with a new client for Savannah River Investigations, Inc.

Unfortunately, he had paid for that mistake by ripping his side again. Four stitches later, he knew his career as a private investigator had ended.

Prematurely.

In the empty kitchen with dusty sun rays shining in, Ming downed some painkillers and dragged himself to the deck.

His smartphone buzzed. A message from Roger, a friend from church, filled the screen. It was long, filled with bullet-points and footnotes, and ended with these words:

ROGER:

> Leaving town tomorrow. Pray for my monthlong visit to Mumbai. But tonight, will come over at six with dinner so you won't starve to death.

Why must everyone baby him?

First his sister, and now one of his best friends?

Sigh.

He turned off his phone and placed it on a window ledge. It was still a bit chilly this late February afternoon, but he was comfortable in his old sweatshirt and shorts.

He climbed into his hammock and grimaced at the pain he still felt in his stomach and side. The internal wounds continued to heal.

Thank God I'm still alive.

He had come a long way since that ambush back in September, but there was a way to go even after half a dozen surgeries. He shouldn't have gone back to work last week, but he had to know whether he could still work.

Well, now I do.

Until he returned to one hundred percent, he couldn't move without gasping for air and experiencing that pain in his side. Injuring old wounds didn't help at all. His being physically unable to do surveillance work killed his business. He could hire someone else to do the work, but he had no money to pay them.

To make it worse, Helen Hu's security firm hadn't given him a definite answer on whether she wanted to buy his company. He needed an infusion of income, or he couldn't run his business and pay the bills.

Being on disability paychecks shamed him.

Ming prayed for relief. When he looked around, he saw his answer. His deck railings, the yard with his charcoal grill in it, the fence, the dune, the beach, the waves, and the ocean beyond, all that reminded him that he lived in a much sought-after oceanfront lot. Taxes and his mortgage were high, and his income was low.

There would be no way for him to stay here, but if he sold it, he could possibly live on the income for a year while he recovered.

He wondered if his sister and Diego would like to buy this house.

Probably not. Diego had said something about wanting a bigger space to hold Bible studies and gatherings.

Ming was thinking about that when he heard a vehicle pull up in his driveway. The street was quiet this afternoon, as few tourists flocked to Tybee Island in the middle of winter, southern weather notwithstanding. He didn't think it was Roger bringing him dinner, because he didn't get off work until five or six in the evening.

Ming couldn't remember if he had locked the front door, and he was sure he should go double-check. But his body didn't move, and his eyelids were too heavy to open. He wondered who was at the door, but this hammock was too comfortable, and the pain medication he'd just taken was kicking in.

~

Sabine Hu figured she could list this cute beach house for three hundred thousand dollars.

Sure can. Easily.

It was an older home, but the exterior looked well-maintained and even recently painted. Cheery yellow walls with white shutters would appeal to double-income no-kid couples looking for weekend getaways on Tybee Island.

The bushes on both sides of the front door had been trimmed down to below the windows. The yard was cleaned up and mowed all the way to the curb where she had parked her SUV.

Nice flat lot. Oceanfront. *What's not to love?*

Sabine stepped into the shade of the front door overhang and pressed the doorbell again.

No answer.

She walked toward the front windows. Those white shutters with the heart cutouts were quaint and screamed female. She wondered who lived with Ming.

She peeked in through the windows. Lots of summer light in the cluttered living room with dark furniture and a big television. The living room itself looked like a man cave.

What a contrast with the feminine exterior.

Sabine knew so little about Aidan Ming Wei, only that he was another private investigator like her sister, Helen. Sabine had seen Ming a couple times at Helen's lavish parties she had held in Savannah to celebrate her successes.

That was all.

They had rarely talked to each other. Sabine had generally been busy keeping Mom out of trouble at parties.

Now Helen had given her a padded envelope to deliver to Ming. It had to be delivered today.

If Sabine didn't have four house showings on Tybee today, she would've said no to being her sister's errand girl.

Yet whenever Helen asked for Sabine's help, she was always there.

Sabine didn't know why she did it. Helen had minions she could have summoned at the wave of her hot-pink fingernails.

But no.

Helen had insisted that this envelope had to be hand-delivered to Ming. Somehow, after all that the sisters had gone through, she still trusted Sabine more than anyone she employed in her private investigation firm, handed down to Helen by their now deceased dad.

Sabine rang the doorbell for a fourth time. She could hear nothing coming from the house. The only sounds surrounding her were the crashing Atlantic Ocean in the backyard, squawks of seabirds above her, and the occasional vehicle engines from the street behind her. It was only February, and tourists thinned out this time of year. Traffic would pick up by May.

Real estate agents could be patient, but it was pushing six o'clock, she hadn't been home for twelve hours, and all Sabine wanted to do now was deliver the envelope, go home, and sit in her hot tub.

The sooner she took care of this matter for Helen, the better.

Sabine found a stone path in the side yard that led to the back of the house. The hedges between this cottage and the neighbor's sprawl had been cut down to a somewhat boxy look. Traditional.

No weeds on the grass. Good.

She almost stepped on an anthill. Not good.

Sabine rounded the corner. The roar of the ocean was louder past the bushes and hedges and might have muffled the doorbell. She came to a deck of weathered pine, and on the deck, under what looked like a retractable fabric awning, was the man himself.

On a hammock, Ming was fast asleep in sweat-shirt and a pair of shorts with faded yellow paint on them. He was buff and tanned, and his shoulders wide and arms long. Sabine wondered if he played football in high school or college.

His legs were pretty cut up and bruised. Old scars. New stitches.

Sabine froze.

Old scars.

Old scars were up and down her legs and thighs too. They were the reason she wore long pants and long skirts when out and about all year long, regardless of how hot it got in coastal Georgia.

And the reason she didn't swim in public anymore.

Sabine clutched her purse, the thick envelope inside. She backed away.

In the hammock, an eye opened. "Sabine?"

CHAPTER TWO

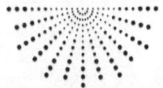

*M*ing blinked. He couldn't remember dozing off. "Sabine Hu, what brings you to the edge of the world?"

Sabine stepped toward him, one hand digging into her tote bag. Ming wondered what she hauled around in that big old bag she had carried everywhere he had seen her.

"Delivery from Helen." Sabine handed him a padded manila envelope.

It looked bulky. Ming lifted a heavy arm, but the envelope was out of reach. He tried to put on a face that showed no pain. "I hate to impose, but you'll have to come closer."

"'Said the spider to the fly.'" Sabine laughed.

"What?"

"Nothing." Sabine put the envelope in Ming's

hand. "You still hurting? I thought you should be healed by now."

"I have new stitches." Ming groaned.

"Injured yourself again?" Sabine stood over the hammock.

"I didn't injure myself. Someone else inflicted this on me."

"Sure. You threw yourself at them, right?"

"Oh yeah. I'm generous that way."

"Well, I'd better be going, but I have a few minutes. Anything I can do for you? Get you a glass of water or something?"

"No, thanks. My friend is bringing dinner, so I'm pampered and taken care of. You're welcome to stay and eat with me."

"Is that an invitation?"

"Never mind. You always turn me down." Ming pried open the envelope and peeked in.

They were in there, as he had expected. Old-school Helen Hu and her color photographs. Nothing digital. Next to the sheath of photographs of their quarry was a stack of twenties. Pocket money to buy donuts and snacks for more surveillance nights sleeping in a van.

I hate this job.

But Ming had no idea what else he could do. His marketing degree from the University of Georgia could be useful somewhere, but he got bored working in the office. He wanted to get out and about. Like Sabine here.

"Say, what percentage do you take when you sell a house?" Ming asked.

Sabine told him right away. "Why?"

"I'm sort of out of work at the moment, and my part-time paycheck doesn't cover my expenses. I'll probably have to sell this house."

Sabine's eyes lit up. Or Ming thought they did.

"This is a cute house," she said. "I'll take a look around to see what we have to work with and give you an estimate. Do some comps and see what sells in this area."

"Take a guess."

"Up and down this street, you're looking at anywhere from three to five and up."

"Cool. I'll take anything a quarter mil and up."

"Not so quick, Ming." Sabine laughed.

Ming stared at her. She had a nice laugh. She didn't crackle and spit like her sister, Helen. Sabine also didn't have a sharp tongue and irritating wit like her older sister. Funny how two siblings could be so different from each other.

Ming liked to think that he and his own sister, Heidi, were much more alike and in tune with each other.

But Sabine and Helen were different. Helen always complained about how introverted Sabine was, how she stuck to herself. Helen had to give her a job of babysitting their mother if only to get Sabine to socialize with their own family members and relatives. Otherwise, Sabine was happy to sit alone at her own home.

But whenever they were in a smaller crowd, perhaps just the two of them, Ming found Sabine easy to talk with. She opened up when she was around him.

Certainly, confidence ran in the Hu family, starting with Mama Hu, the widow and majority owner of Hu Private Investigations, Inc. It had been Mama Hu who had changed the name of their firm to Hu Knows, Inc.

And if Helen and Mama Hu agreed, Ming's own company would become a branch of Hu Knows very soon.

But I digress.

So. Sabine.

Standing right here over my hammock looking—

Pretty?

Maybe it was the sunlight on her hair, creating something like a glow on her head.

"Hello?" Sabine waved a hand over his eyes.

"Oh sorry. Painkillers." *Yep. When embarrassed for staring, blame something.* "So. Dinner?"

"You poor, lonely dude."

"That I am. You have a date tonight? That's it,

isn't it?" Ming wondered if Sabine dated at all. Unlike her sister, Sabine seemed to keep to herself. "I'm glad you got rid of the cane."

Sabine bristled.

"I don't mean—ah. You know me, Sabine. Foot in mouth. Forgive me?"

"Sure. Shut up and maybe you won't have to apologize so much."

"Do you really forgive me?"

"Yeah. Cane jokes. Heard it all."

"If you do really forgive me, then it's no trouble eating dinner with me."

"You're persistent."

"We won't be alone, you know. My friend, Roger, is coming over."

"I don't know your friend."

"You know me."

"The pain in the neck?" Sabine laughed.

Ming felt hurt. Sure, they joked a lot, but what she said hurt. "Am I really a pain in the neck to you?"

"I don't know why I said that. I don't even work with you."

"Your sister said something about me?" Ming tried to read Sabine's face. He couldn't see anything incriminating. If Helen had misgivings about him, she might not buy Savannah River Investigations, Inc.

Right now, he wanted it sold, preferably to Helen. He could work for her, get a salary, benefits, healthcare, dental, 401K, the works.

He'd never have to bother looking for new clients again. Helen's company, Hu Knows, had clients everywhere, even in Europe and South America. He could travel the world and not worry about income.

"Nothing at all. Helen and I don't talk about each other's work."

Ming tried to dig deeper. "I'm surprised that you don't have a share in Hu Knows."

"I sold my share to Mom when it was still named Hu Private Investigations. I've never been interested. I'd rather sell houses."

"Helen said you wanted to do your own thing."

"That's right. Besides, we can't have both of us in the same company. We'd be tearing each other's hair out."

Ming chuckled. "I'd hate to see your lovely hair —ah..."

Sabine shrugged. "I probably need a haircut."

"No. I like it long. Just like that."

"You like my hair long?" Sabine asked.

"I do." Ming left it at that.

He thought of inviting her again to dinner, but he decided not to press. It would only turn Sabine away. She was comfortable with him, and they were friends of sorts, thanks to their connection to Helen.

That was all.

If he were to help her gain more confidence about herself, the last thing he should do was shoot down that very fragile self-esteem.

At the same time, he was trying to help her as a friend. Sabine was nice and all, but probably not his type. He was outgoing and fun to be with—if he didn't say so himself—but Sabine was quiet and hated big groups. *Never the twain shall meet.*

Perhaps it was their upbringing. Ming had grown up in a small family, so most of his company were friends and colleagues. Since his parents had passed away, he hadn't gone home much to Toronto to see his relatives, and they hadn't come down to Savannah to visit him. Everyone had their own lives, and no one had suggested possible family reunions.

Sabine's family, on the other hand, was mostly in the Savannah and Charleston area. Some of their Hu relatives were in metro Atlanta, but that was only five hours of driving from coastal Georgia.

They could get together more often, especially when Mama Hu and Helen threw their many cele-brations year round. There was always something going on in the Hu family, and friends were invited. To Mama Hu, friends were a source of business.

And business at Hu Knows, and all its previous names, was very good.

Very, very good.

"Drifting off again?" Sabine asked. "Maybe you should get back to your nap. I'll be going now. See you later. And you can tell Helen that I made the delivery."

"All right. Thanks." He waved the envelope at her. "Your sister does trust you, doesn't she?"

"I wish she had someone in her company she trusted more than me so that I didn't have to do errands for her like this."

"I hear you. Unpaid, even."

"Not that. I'm in the area. Had several houses to show. But even though she's my sister, I don't like to make deliveries of unknown things, you know. Like, what's in that envelope?"

"Point taken." Ming wasn't going to show Sabine the photographs he had received.

He shifted in his hammock and tried to get up. "I'm rude! I forgot to invite you to sit down or offer you a drink. What will Mama Hu say?"

"Don't worry about it. I'm leaving, anyway." She rattled a bunch of keys in her hand.

"Maybe dinner another time."

"Maybe." Sabine stepped off the deck.

"When can we talk about this house?" Ming asked as she waved.

"If you're serious, call me."

"I'm serious."

"Okay." Sabine swiped her iPhone. "Monday morning at eight or Friday at four. I can call you if there's a cancellation, but my calendar is full the rest of the week."

"People look at houses in the winter?"

"All year round in Savannah and on Tybee. About now, families start thinking of the next school year, you know."

Ming flinched as he eased off the hammock and reached for his iPhone just as Sabine's own phone rang.

CHAPTER THREE

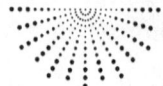

"*T*hirty minutes?" Sabine sighed. "I can't make it in thirty minutes. It's rush hour right now, and the house is in Savannah. I'm in a meeting on Tybee at the moment—What? You'll wait? See, Mr. Atkinson—Oh, your wife wants the house badly? Hold on a sec."

She walked across the yard toward the fence and ocean as she checked the listing. Twenty-nine-million-dollar nineteenth-century stucco. She'd been trying to sell that house for months. The owner had kept lowering the price to the point that even she could pick it up herself.

Then again, the renovation would be a killer. She had no time for that. She had some historian friends who would be interested, but their historical societies didn't have enough funds for this house. So on the market it had stayed.

"I understand, Mr. Atkinson. How about tomorrow morning? When do you leave town?" Sabine listened.

The man wouldn't let up. Something about paying for half the house up front caught her attention. What would her commission be?

She mentally calculated herself into saying yes. "If you give me an hour, I think I can make it. See you then."

She hung up, spun around, and met Ming's glare.

"It'll be dark in an hour," he said.

"The street is well lit," Sabine countered.

"Haven't you read the news about real estate agents getting killed after dark?"

"Savannah is a safe town. You should know, being a PI and all."

"No city is ever safe." Ming lifted his green shirt to reveal a giant bandage across the side of his stomach. "The safe town of Savannah happened to me. So don't tell me it's okay for you to wander around in the dark."

"Last I checked, I didn't hire you to do security for me, Ming." Sabine put away her iPhone. Better get going if she wanted to make it to the last-minute house showing.

Atkinson had talked to her several times this week, so it wasn't like she was unfamiliar with the out-of-towner. He had said he was Floridian, his wife was eight months pregnant, and he just got a job at the hospital in Savannah.

Sounds legit.

"Besides, I have a new Glock." Sabine wondered why she mentioned it. Maybe she thought that Ming would understand.

"As in a firearm?" Ming looked at her in disbelief.

"No, as in a designer handbag." Sabine rolled her eyes.

"And you have a license to carry?"

"You mock me, Ming. Do you have something against Glocks? Just because my sister carries a Sig, it doesn't mean I should too."

"I'm asking. Literally asking. To know. Not to mock. Besides, I use both. Want me to give you some pointers?"

Sabine lifted her eyebrows. *No need to be defensive.*

"I think I can figure it out," she said, giving away nothing.

"Figure it out?" Ming hobbled across the floor-board toward Sabine.

"Don't hurt yourself." Sabine could feel his height looming over her.

"How new is your Glock?" Ming cringed as he held his side.

"It just arrived today. I ordered it from the same place Helen does. Next-day delivery."

"And it's in your purse?"

"In the trunk of my SUV."

"What a handy place to put it."

"Mocking me again." There was so much Ming didn't know about her, but Sabine wasn't about to tell all.

"No, no. Do you know how to use it?"

"Why are you asking me all these questions?" Sabine felt perturbed. "Did Helen tell you something I don't know?"

"She's the shooter. You're the model."

"Was." It was a long story Sabine didn't want to get into. "What are you implying? Are you insulting my pink Glock?"

"Pink?" Ming began to choke, like he couldn't breathe.

Sabine watched him carefully, in case she needed to apply the Heimlich on him. She'd done it before on a client's son, though Ming was a whole foot taller than she was, and his girth was probably too big for her to wrap her arms around.

"Sorry. Something in my throat." Ming stopped coughing.

"Like your foot?"

"Okay, let me get this straight. Sabine, you have an unknown house showing tonight. You have a Glock, but you've never used it."

Sabine was annoyed Ming was at her heels. "You don't know me."

"Hold that thought." Ming hobbled to his back door.

"Poor thing, you. Maybe you should rest. If I need help, I'll call you. How's that?"

Ming turned his head. "Stay put, Sabine. Promise? I'll be right back."

Sabine sighed. Her phone pinged her a few times. Text messages from other clients.

When it rains...

Before she knew it, Ming reappeared, slamming his door shut. He had on a pair of boots.

"Let's go," Ming said, limping down the steps.

CHAPTER FOUR

*H*is aftershave smelled amazing. That was the bad news.

He was riding shotgun. That was the good news.

Somehow Sabine felt calmer having a PI around, but he was injured, had a big old bandage around his stomach, walked like he could collapse anytime, and had practically insulted her shiny, new pink Glock.

What's wrong with men these days?

Okay, Sabine was driving. That put her in the control seat, right?

She glanced at Mr. Polo Aftershave in the passenger seat, texting on his phone.

Tap, tap, tap.

Whatever he was doing was none of Sabine's

business, but she wondered if it had anything to with complaining to Helen about her.

As far as she knew, Helen and Ming were tight. They were both single, and Sabine wouldn't put it past Helen to go out with Ming. Good for her. Helen worked very hard and deserved a good man in her life.

Ming was a good man.

Always up front, never manipulative. *What you see is what you get.*

That's the kind of man I—

Forget it.

"Wow. Just wow." Those were the first words Ming had spoken since Sabine crossed into downtown Savannah.

"Something wrong?" she asked.

"Nothing, except that the perp we caught for the police back in September has been released on bail and disappeared."

"Meaning?"

"Meaning I failed. We failed. I got shot for nothing. Daljeet died for nothing. Camden got fired for nothing." Ming leaned his head back against the leather headrest.

"I saw something about that in the news, but it has nothing to do with my sister, right?"

"No, but the success of that was supposed to help me sell my company to her."

"So sorry." Sabine parked as closely as possible to the historic home.

It meant her car was only about twenty feet from the stoplight of a deserted street. The last Savannah square was a block away, and she could see the tall overhanging live oak branches some ninety or a hundred feet in the air, reaching toward this block in the dusky evening.

Sabine looked around the area. No other vehicles on this street. It was, for all practical purposes, desolate.

She didn't realize she was making any kind of noise.

"You okay?" Ming asked.

Sabine nodded. "I don't usually show homes in the evenings, if I can help it. Safety first, you know. But Mr. Atkinson sounded genuine."

"The best cons always do." Ming reached out and wrapped his palm around her right hand. It calmed her down some.

"I'm okay." Sabine pulled her hand away.

"I'm sorry. I didn't mean—Look, I think we should leave. It's not safe with just us here."

Sabine snapped down her door lock. All the doors locked at once.

"How's that going to help?" Ming's eyes seemed to be everywhere.

Sabine dialed Mr. Atkinson's number on her cell phone.

"The number you're trying to reach is not in service."

Huh?

"I heard that," Ming said.

Sabine hung up. She closed her eyes.

"Want me to drive, ma'am? I think I can handle this Mercedes."

"You're going to make me get out?" Sabine's eyes were huge. "We can't switch seats without stepping out."

"Better not. So let's go?"

Sabine nodded. She started the ignition. Pulled away from the curb.

"Another no-show." She shrugged.

"Maybe he saw that you weren't alone and he left."

"But why? What have I done to anyone? I only sell houses. Everyday stuff, if you ask me."

"We'll know more once we have a better idea of what's going on. Maybe you can tell me about all your clients from the last year or so?"

Sabine laughed. "Many satisfied customers, if you want to know. I'm a small fry, Ming. No enemies."

"Your sister has enemies."

Sabine couldn't respond to that.

Silence hung between them for a while as Sabine drove Ming home. He shouldn't have come with her. Now she had to drop him off. Then again, she felt safe with Ming around. She hadn't felt safe in—

I have Jesus.

God has always been with me.

"I hope this won't be too much of a drive for you to take me home to Tybee. Least I can do is give you dinner. Roger should've dropped it off while we were driving around."

Sabine glanced at Ming.

"We'll sit on my porch and listen to the ocean," Ming added. "You don't get that from your porch, do you?"

"I don't have a porch. I have a rooftop terrace."

"No yard?"

"No yard. I wish I had one." Sabine often thought of that whenever she showed a house with a yard to prospective buyers. "Someday I'll buy a house that has a backyard of some sort. Plant some flowers. I'm no gardener, but I'll pay someone."

"Interested in buying an oceanfront beach house with a nice little yard you can plant azaleas in?"

"Ha." It might beat her view of the Savannah River.

"Tiny starter house for you and your future beau."

"It'll be a long time."

"One never knows. Our lives are in God's hands."

"You can say that again. I've been through enough to know that if it wasn't for God's mercy, I wouldn't have lived."

"That makes two of us. So where do you go to church?" Ming asked.

"I'm not a member anywhere. I visit a few churches. Rotate among them."

"Don't you want a church home? Where you can belong?"

"I read my Bible." Sabine meant it as a protest.

"I do too. But the Bible says not to forsake the assembling of believers to worship God."

"I haven't found a church I like and want to stay in. I like them all, it seems. I tithe everywhere."

"If you're visiting churches, want to visit mine?" Ming asked.

Sabine let him wait while she mulled it over. What harm was there? "Where's your church?"

"In a riverboat on the Savannah River."

"Seriously?" Sabine parked her SUV. "Let me guess. It's called the Riverboat Church, as opposed to a riverboat casino."

Ming remained serious. "No gambling allowed.

It's Riverside Chapel. The pastor is married to my sister, and they should be home from their honeymoon next week. His dad is preaching in his place this weekend. He's funny. Do you like funny sermons?"

"You can read that in so many ways," Sabine said.

"I mean Pastor Flores the Senior makes me laugh. And it hurts my stomach when I do that."

"I could use something light in my life right now." Sabine regretted her words the moment they left her mouth.

"Me too. Pain therapy, you know."

"Tell me about it." Sabine didn't get out of the car.

Ming opened his passenger side door. "Do your legs still hurt?"

"They have pins and needles, so to speak. Titanium bolts and rods."

"I'm surprised you can talk about stuff like that so easily."

"Why not? I have to live with this. If not for God, I would never walk again." Sabine felt uncomfortable with Ming staring at her with those brown eyes. She stiffened. *Shields up!*

"And here I am moaning and groaning," Ming said as he got out of the car.

"I haven't heard you complain."

"When nobody's around, I have my pity party. Join me?"

Sabine grinned. "Been there. Done that."

"All right, I'll take your rain check," Ming said.

"For what?"

"Dinner."

"Why don't you invite Helen instead?" Sabine wasn't sure why she even said that. "She's more your type."

"And what's my type?"

"Noisy."

"I don't want her. I want to have dinner with you—Oops, that came out wrong."

"Don't worry about it." Sabine brushed it off. It was probably his meds. "Take it easy, Ming, and don't overdose on your painkillers."

"I'll try not to." Ming started walking. Then he turned back and came to the driver's side. "Do you have an alarm system in your house?"

"Everyone does. Why?"

"And you arm it at night, I assume?" Ming was all business.

"Yes. Why?"

"I want to be sure."

He cares?

Sabine laughed. "Sometimes people don't show up for house showings. Happens."

"Yeah, and sometimes their phone number is no longer in service at the same time."

Sabine sighed. "That is odd."

"Tell me all about this Atkinson and his wife, and I'll look into it."

"I'm not hiring you."

"Pro bono."

"Why?"

"I can't help myself."

Sabine thought for a minute. No harm done, right? "All right. I'll send all that info to you later. For the record though, I think it'll be a waste of your time. A useless exercise."

"I need to know." Ming waved.

"Step back a bit. I don't want to run over your feet backing out of your driveway."

Ming laughed. "Then you'll have to babysit me instead of Mama Hu."

"She'll love you for that!"

CHAPTER FIVE

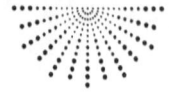

*B*y the time Sabine reached her penthouse overlooking the Savannah River, it was dark outside and she was famished.

She opened the refrigerator door to find nothing to eat but some cheesecake left over from the last dinner party Helen had thrown at her house two blocks away.

Oh, three days ago.

She sniffed the cheesecake. It smelled fine. In fact, it smelled edible.

Carrying the dessert plate and a fork, Sabine padded across her wood floor toward her rooftop terrace. Her legs hurt a little climbing up the spiral stairs, but just a few more steps up, and she'd be outside heading for her lounge chair looking up at the stars above Savannah.

She stopped at the door.

Someone was sitting on her favorite lounge chair between her hot tub and her swimming pool.

"Mom! What are you doing here?" Sabine walked gingerly to a deck chair. She sat down.

On Mom's lap was a tub of Sabine's favorite ice cream. Almond and fudge with bits of chocolate. In the tub was a spoon.

Plus saliva.

"I'm spending the night. Is that okay?" Mom sniffled.

"Sure. You have the key. Anytime." This three-level penthouse, renovated from an 1890 building, was the clincher that had made Sabine give up her share of the family business.

If she had done this before Dad passed away, he would never have approved. Dad had wanted both of his daughters to own the multinational private investigation firm, whether or not Sabine had any interest in it at all.

It had taken a while for Sabine to get out of the family business long before that fatal wreck she had been in that had killed one of the company associates.

The family hadn't wanted her to leave. She persisted. She wanted out. She didn't do anything in the company anyway, having spent more of her time in the European modeling circuit. Primarily, she had been a leg model.

Then, on that two-week vacation celebrating Mom's birthday in Savannah, Helen and Sabine were on their way to the hair salon with a coworker, when Helen suddenly cut someone off on East Bay Street, turned the wrong way onto a one-way street, and swerved to avoid a dump truck. Her BMW went airborne, landed upside down, and crushed the passenger side with Sabine in it.

Helen's coworker in the backseat had died instantly.

Sabine had spent the next year in and out of the hospital having her legs reconstructed, and crying rivers of regret that her modeling career had ended due to Helen's careless driving.

Ironically, Helen had walked away from the five-vehicle pileup unscathed. Helen's bruises had healed before Sabine was discharged from the hospital.

To this day, Sabine didn't know the details of that entire episode. She only knew that it was a miracle she walked again. It was a miracle, indeed.

Thank you, Jesus!

They sat in silence as Sabine watched Mom scoop another dollop of ice cream. She polished it off, licked the spoon, and plunged it back into the tub.

Sabine lost her appetite. She put down her cheesecake. "Tell me what happened, Mom."

"It's Leung."

Oh dear. Boyfriend trouble again.

"Is it Leung the Older or Leung the Younger?"

"Leung the Both." Mom ate more ice cream. "His dad said he can't marry me. Why not, I ask you? Why not? I'm only fifty-nine!"

"Mom, you're sixty-four."

"That can't be right."

"You had me when you were thirty-five years old, remember? I'm twenty-nine this year."

Mom ate two more scoops of ice cream.

"You could get ill on that." For emphasis, Sabine pointed to the tub of ice cream.

"I like ice cream. Your ice cream. Helen's options are horrid. All low fat, full of saccharin and whatnots. You have the best kind. Ooh, my tummy hurts." Mom leaned back on the lounge chair. The tub of ice cream with the spoon sticking out of it sat precariously on top of her stomach. For a petite lady, Mom was in pretty good shape, except when she had boyfriend troubles.

"See what I'm saying, Mom?" Sabine shook her head. "You're getting ill from too much dessert."

"I shouldn't have tried her bacon-and-cheese ice cream."

Sabine gagged. "You had a progressive dessert party all by yourself?"

"Helen was home. She's having some sort of a meeting. I wasn't invited."

"I'm sorry."

"It's about that early release. That September case."

"Bail, Mom. Not early release."

"Whatever. Point is, the guy is bad. He might come after your sister."

Sabine stretched her legs. "How does that have anything to do with either Leung?"

"Leung's dad said my work is too dangerous for his son, and he doesn't want him to marry me."

Sure. "Did he say anything about the fact that you're twenty years older than your boyfriend?"

"Fifteen."

"Whatever." Mom had never been good in math. Sabine let it go. She was exhausted, tired, and had a house showing at nine in the morning. She really needed to get to bed.

But here's Mom.

"Want to watch a movie?" Sabine asked. "It might take your mind off the entire Leung family."

"Yes."

"But first we'll pray, all right? Let's ask God for His perfect will for your love life." Sabine scooted her deck chair closer to Mom.

"For you too, baby girl."

Baby girl.

Sabine hated being called that anymore, but Mom was having her moment of angst. Sometimes she called her daughters stuff like that when she longed for days gone by, days when Sabine and her sister had been little girls, when life was easy, and Dad had come home every night alive to happy family dinners.

Mom's voice softened. "Maybe God will bring you a good husband."

"I don't want nor need a husband, Mom. I'm very happy alone."

"It's no fun being alone. Ask me how I know." Mom dug around the tub of ice cream.

"Some of us are meant to be alone. I don't want anyone messing up my house and life."

"Ah, the irony." Mom smiled. "You're a good judge of character, and yet you can't find a mate."

"Mate? Mom!"

"Don't you want to be married?"

"Nope."

"Have kids?"

"Nope."

"Grow old together with someone..." Mom's voice trailed off. She burst into tears.

Sabine descended on Mom. She hugged her and

patted her back. "It's going to be okay, Mom. Dad has gone to heaven."

"Why did he leave me here to suffer? To be alone?"

"You're not alone. You have Helen and me."

Me.

Suddenly it became clear to Sabine why she hadn't died in the wreck three years ago.

CHAPTER SIX

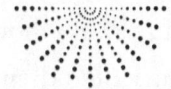

*M*ing had no part in the safe rescue of the senator's daughter, but Helen Hu had sent him a party invitation nonetheless.

So there he was, a teetotaler amid a sea of drinkers, rubbing shoulders with business associates of Hu Knows, Inc., and making Mama Hu laugh, as per his usual interaction with the matriarch of the Hu family.

Speaking of family, where's Sabine?

Ming spent half the evening looking for her, and he didn't know why. Everyone said she was around. He knew that Sabine would be close by Mama Hu, just in case the lady had too much to drink and her daughters had to escort her off the premises—or to her bedroom upstairs in the swanky turn-of-thecentury mansion on Bull Street. When sober, Mama Hu was the gatekeeper in the PI firm, with nothing going past her and nothing escaping her scrutiny, although, truth be told, most of the day-to-day operations had now been left in her oldest daughter's hands.

Still, Mama Hu knew how to throw lavish success parties, as she called them.

Soirees like this one.

Right in her own home.

Ming knew that Mama Hu lived with Helen in this house. He also knew that they had purchased this house two years ago, with Sabine as the buyer's agent. Her commission must've been pretty good for this three-million-dollar historic home. He tapped the floor with his polished dress shoes and made a mental note to ask Sabine about the floor.

The floor? Whatever for?

He heard a familiar laugh. Sort of a mix of a chuckle and a true laugh. Unfortunately, the source came not from Sabine but from two people. Helen and Mama Hu were cutting it up with some guys in designer tuxedos.

Then he spotted Sabine through the hallway, between some sort of old sofa and a painting hanging on the wall. She had her head down, but she was tall enough for Ming to follow her as she made her way behind a potted plant.

How apropos.

Ming put down his mineral water on a passing server's tray. He straightened his bow tie and made his way toward Sabine. He wasn't sure what he was going to say to her, but first he had to get to her.

For some reason, he had to see her.

His cufflinks brushed past the potted plants.

Sabine was dressed in a royal-blue silk dress that covered her from neck to toe. It was modest but flowingly pretty. Her long hair was lifted up into a chignon, and her neck was long and smooth.

She was leaning against a pillar, two thumbs on her iPhone. She didn't look up, and Ming was sure she wasn't aware of who was around her. He walked as quietly as he could on the plush carpet, hardly breathing. When he reached her, he saw the gold necklace around her neck, a cross hanging off it.

He didn't remember seeing that necklace before, and Ming had fancied himself to be an observant guy.

Swiftly, he yanked that iPhone out of her hands.

"Hey!" Sabine looked up. "Ming."

"Hi, Sabine." He pocketed her iPhone in his tuxedo jacket.

"Give it back." Sabine reached for the pocket.

Ming moved his hip back and away from her.

Sabine stepped forward. She must be wearing super high heels, because they were eye to eye, and

Ming was over six feet tall. Her hand was on his pocket, and Ming's hand clasped hers.

They froze.

Ming didn't let go of her hand. She didn't pull away like she had done in the SUV the evening before.

Somewhere in the background, the string quintet started to play soft medleys again. People's voices muffled some of the notes. Here behind the pillar, surrounded by people's backs, Ming could see how Sabine had found a somewhat private space.

Ming lifted Sabine's hand to his lips. He kissed it gently.

"Why did you do that?" Sabine asked.

Ming shrugged. He had no words. He really didn't know why he had kissed her hand. His other hand went to her face. Her cheek and chin felt smooth beneath his fingers.

A waltz began to play.

"Do you waltz?" Ming asked quietly.

"Not often. Do you?"

"When undercover."

Sabine smiled. "That so?"

"May I have this dance?" Ming wasn't sure why he asked. It seemed like he was saying things he couldn't reason and doing things he couldn't explain.

"No one else is dancing, Ming."

"I know. I'm not sure what I was thinking."

"Besides, neither of us is good at it."

"You remember from Mama Hu's last ball." Ming couldn't remember when that had been, but he recalled that they were both there.

"Yep."

"We'll improvise."

Sabine laughed. "You're not drunk, are you?"

"I don't drink."

"Hmm. My kind of guy."

"Am I?" Ming wrapped his free arm around Sabine's waist.

"I don't know. All I know is there's no room here to dance." Sabine put her other hand on Ming's shoulder.

"We won't take up a large footprint."

"We'll go dizzy going around in tight circles."

Ming laughed and couldn't stop, and he gripped his stomach. "Ouch. Can't. Laugh."

"This is when laughter can kill." Sabine stepped closer.

Ming felt a hand in his tuxedo pocket. He was in pain, so he let her go.

"I guess I won't report that my iPhone was stolen." Sabine waved her phone at Ming.

Ming didn't share the joke. His stomach hurt. Badly.

Lord, help me.

"You okay?" Sabine felt his forehead.

"It's not my forehead. It's my—I just need to sit down a bit."

"And no more dancing," Sabine said.

"We didn't even begin." Ming followed Sabine down the same hallway he had seen her come through.

CHAPTER SEVEN

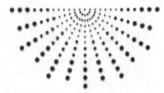

Down the hallway, there was an alcove where a set of glass doors led them into a small sitting room. People were sitting down, talking.

Ming checked the faces. None of them was in Helen's inner circle. Good. The last thing he wanted was for them to report his poor health to her, thereby negating any efforts he was trying to make toward the sale of Savannah River Investigations to Hu Knows.

He sat down where Sabine pointed.

"Would you like a glass of water?" she asked.

"Yes, please." Ming rummaged through his pockets for something for the pain. He had stopped taking prescription painkillers because they masked his discomfort.

Sabine returned pretty quickly, goblet of water and a paper napkin in her hand.

"Thank you." Ming swallowed his over-the-counter generic acetaminophen. It was then that he realized Sabine was sitting right next to him, watching him.

"Maybe we should check your bandage," Sabine said.

"We? Nope. Don't worry about it, okay? I just laughed too hard."

Sabine nodded. Then she put a hand on his arm. He could feel her warmth through the tuxedo sleeve. When he looked at her face, tears pooled in her eyes.

"Hey..." He wiped those tears with his fingers. "What's going on?"

"It's going to be okay."

Is she telling me or asking me? "Oh yes. Don't worry about it."

"Even if you're in pain."

"No worries. It's only temporary. It'll heal."

Sabine's tears didn't stop.

All Ming had was a paper napkin that had come with the goblet. He handed it to Sabine, who dabbed her own eyes with it.

What did I just trigger?

Ming couldn't be sure. That was over-the-top concern for his wounds from someone he was just getting to know. It had to be more than that. What, then? He took a stab at guessing. "How long has it been?"

"Three years and some months."

I knew it.

It was no longer about his stomach wounds, but about Sabine's own healing.

Ming was amazed at the number of surgeries that Sabine had gone through to reconstruct her shattered legs. Helen had told him all about it. Whenever they had downtime while working together, she'd talk about her family.

"Do your legs still hurt?" Ming asked.

"Sometimes."

"When you walk?"

"When I climb stairs. Or run."

"At other times it hurts more because it wasn't your fault that it happened." Ming didn't know how those words came out of his mouth, but came out they did.

Sabine nodded.

Ming's hand went around Sabine's shoulders. When he lifted his arm, his stitches stretched and pinched him something fierce, but he didn't care. The OTC pain meds should kick in anytime now.

He wanted to put his hand on the base of Sabine's neck, but he didn't. He kept his hand on her shoulders, where she was fully clothed.

Beyond the door, the crowd hadn't thinned. Chatter, laughter, background music. All white noise.

Helen and Mama Hu were nowhere in sight. Well, Ming couldn't see anyone in the crowd from the disadvantage of sitting on a low couch.

Ming turned his attention back to Sabine. He felt a connection between then. His pastor friend, Diego Flores—it was still hard to imagine him as his brother-in-law now—had told him that seeking God first was always the wisest thing to do.

What should I say to Sabine, Lord?

In a flash, he was angry at Sabine's sister. He hadn't expected to think that. He knew this reaction wasn't from God. It was from himself.

"Helen should never have put you in danger," Ming whispered harshly. "You were collateral damage."

"I'm always collateral damage."

"Not to me." Ming lifted her chin. "You know you can talk to me anytime. We're in the same boat. We can pray for each other. Help each other. Are we buddies?"

Sabine nodded.

Ming wished she hadn't. He couldn't believe himself. He had asked her to be his buddy. But he didn't look at her as a buddy.

No. He wanted more.

He wasn't sure if they could have more. It would get complicated. Helen might think he was trying to become a family friend so that she would look more favorably at their business transaction. Helen might think—

What do I care what Helen thinks?

"I'm sorry for what happened to you," Ming said. "Wish I was there when you needed someone."

"I have Jesus," Sabine said.

"Yes, I do too."

"God was with me all the way through the surgeries, the rehab, the physical therapies." Sabine managed a smile.

Ming had come to like her smiles. "With me too, though what I went through was nothing like what you suffered."

"And nothing I went through could compare to what Christ suffered at the cross for us."

"I like that perspective, Sabine."

"It's the only way to survive tough times, as you know."

"Right." Ming wasn't sure what else to say to her in a room full of strangers.

They were sitting alone on this couch, yes, and everyone else minded their own business. He and Sabine had a morsel of privacy, and it was a good thing they weren't by themselves. That would be inappropriate, and he'd never hear the end of that from Diego and Heidi. Still, he didn't feel like they were alone enough to talk about God.

And yet they had.

Sabine was a Christian, and so was he. It was inevitable that they'd talk about God.

Out of the heart the mouth speaks.

After all, God had helped both of them through their physical trials.

"You were at Savannah Memorial, weren't you?" Ming asked.

"Yeah. Stuck on a hospital bed longer than I wanted to be."

"So was I."

"We have a lot in common," Sabine said quietly.

What else do we have in common?

"It's no fun being in and out of hospitals, if you want to know what I think." Sabine shrugged. "I'd rather forget all of that."

Ming nodded. "Me too. But like you said, God was with us."

"I'm forever grateful He was." Sabine took a deep breath. "Well, thanks for sitting with me. How's your stomach feeling now?"

"Better." Ming wanted to leave his arm around Sabine's shoulders, but he sensed that the moment was over. He wasn't sure what Sabine had made of that. He didn't want to turn her away for any reason, however small. More than wanting her to sell his house, he wanted to know her more.

"I'm glad. I'll pray for God to heal you," Sabine said.

"Thank you. Much appreciated."

"Maybe you should take time off."

"That's what the doc said." Ming sighed.

"However?"

Might as well say it, Ming thought. "I need the work."

"If we stage your house, it'll sell at a higher price. Maybe that can hold you over until you heal."

"You haven't been inside my house." Ming tipped his head. "How do you know my house is worth anything?"

"I can tell from the comps in your area. The location is perfect for all sorts of buyers."

"Wish I could afford to keep it."

"A house is a house is a house."

Sabine said it in such a singsong way that Ming started to laugh, causing his hand to drop to his tummy. "Ouch."

"Maybe you should go home. Lie down. Rest," Sabine suggested.

"I will." Ming breathed deeply. The slight pulling pain allayed. He tried to smile. "And you, Sabine, don't worry about your past. Leave it in the able hands of God. Like my mother used to say, there's a reason God put eyes in front of our heads. We don't look back except to remember the faithfulness of God. We press on."

Sabine's lips quivered.

Ming thought her eyes were glistening again. "Hey, that was supposed to encourage you."

"You're a kind man, Ming," Sabine said.

Kind?

Is that all you think of me?

CHAPTER EIGHT

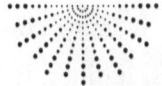

A *riverboat church. Interesting.*

Sabine had never been in one before.

She walked up the ramp with other churchgoers. In slacks and a simple blouse, she fitted in with some of the crowd. The rest were either in suits or tee shirts and jeans.

Riverside Chapel's come-as-you-are policy seemed to be an attempt to attract tourists in downtown Savannah, particularly those walking about the riverfront on Sunday mornings.

Sabine had been having breakfast alone on her rooftop terrace, the mild February sun shining down on her, a soft wind picking up across the Savannah River from Hutchinson Island, when she looked down River Street and saw two riverboats.

People were entering both riverboats. Sabine

wondered if one of them might be the venue for Ming's church. Google confirmed it as Riverside Chapel.

Fifty minutes later, Sabine was standing outside the dining room.

"Good morning! Welcome to Riverside Chapel." A smiling woman about Sabine's age, but shorter than she was, handed her a flyer that turned out to be the morning's program. There was nothing more welcoming than a genuine smile on a greeter's face. There were other churches she had visited where it felt like she was attending a funeral.

"Thank you. This is so pretty." Sabine ran a finger over the watercolor design on the printout.

"Thanks. I did that. You look new. Have you been here before?" She extended her hand. "I'm Abilene Dupree."

"Sabine Hu. First time here." She shook Abilene's hand. "A friend invited me. Aidan Ming Wei? Ming?"

"Oh yeah. There's only one Ming we know." Abilene looked around. "I don't see him, but he should be here somewhere. Saw him this morning in Sunday School. Why don't you have a seat, and I'll let him know?"

"Okay. Sit anywhere?"

"Anywhere you want. I sit in the back because I stand here until the choir sings, so if you want to sit

with me, I'm at that table by the window over there."
Abilene pointed.

Sabine wasn't sure which table she was pointing
to, and Abilene had to greet the next people in line.
Sabine stepped to the side, thinking she'd just sit
anywhere.

"Sabine."

Ming.

Sabine turned toward the voice. The first thing
that caught her eye was Ming's vest. It was a dark-
ish-chocolate color with leather trim. "Nice vest.
Looks good on you."

"Glad you like it."

"How are you? How are your stitches?"

"Better." Ming's hand rose toward Sabine's, as if
he wanted to hold hers, but then he dipped both
hands into his dress pants pockets instead. "What
do you think of our church?"

"Is this a permanent location?"

"Hope not. All we need is a storm, and it'll wash
out to sea."

"But not today. Which table is Abilene's? I'm
sitting with her."

Ming scrunched up his face. "You don't want to
sit with me?"

"I asked her first." Abilene stepped toward
them. "Ming, are you going to invite your friend to
lunch? I need to text Piper to reserve seats."

"Lunch?" Sabine asked. They hadn't started church, and these people were planning lunch?

"We go from here to lunch," Abilene said, as if church and lunch were part and parcel of Sundays. Then she was off again, wishing the next person coming in a hearty good morning.

"Would you like to have lunch with us?" Ming asked softly as he ushered Sabine to Abilene's table. "Piper's Place."

"Sure. I like their brioche sandwiches."

"Nothing I don't like there." Ming pulled back a seat for Sabine.

A nice gentleman.

He sat down next to her.

Sabine wasn't sure what to think of that. She had felt comfortable with Ming in the months she had known him through Helen's and Mom's circle of friends. She had known he was a Christian. But they had been acquaintances then.

Friday night had changed something in their friendship, not when he had kissed her hand or called her a buddy, but when she realized how much they had in common through something as morbid as their physical injuries and recoveries. Of all the men she had come in contact with, Ming hadn't even been on her radar.

What radar?

Sabine tried not to think too much about it.

There were no possibilities. If not for Helen's business dealings, Sabine wouldn't have crossed paths with Ming. Next week, it was business again when Sabine prepared to put Ming's house on the market.

She felt his breath on her left ear.

"What are you thinking?" Ming asked as the piano started to play.

"How to sell your house," Sabine blurted. *Well, I was getting to that part.*

"Let's leave business at home, shall we? I'm glad you decided to visit our church this morning."

Sabine nodded. "It's not far from my house."

"Maybe you'll come back again when Diego— Pastor Flores—is back in town. I want you to meet my sister, Heidi."

Meet your sister?

Sabine tried not to read too much into it.

CHAPTER NINE

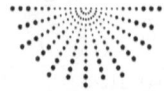

"We'll have to declutter this house." Sabine opened the last door on the hallway to yet another small room.

It was the size of her own walk-in closet, but it would do for a guest or a child's bedroom. Kids weren't going to stay indoors all day anyway. Not when there was a whole beach in the backyard.

"And this room, especially." She stepped over a pair of mismatched flip-flops on the floor toward a long twin-size bed pushed up against a wood-paneled wall that was severely outdated. Next to the unmade bed was a crate for a side table below a window.

She stood at the window.

Zero view.

She could hear the ocean, but the storage shed

in the side yard outside the window pretty much blocked out the bushes, dunes, and any ocean view.

"I was going to clean up this place before you came, but I got called away," Ming said from the door.

"I'm not accusing you of anything." Sabine turned toward him. "I'm going through the things we need to do before we list this house."

"Okay. Fair enough." Ming straightened up, winced, and put a palm on his stomach.

"Would you like to sit down? I can do the tour on my own."

"No worries. It comes and goes." Behind him, lining the rest of the wall in this small room, were boxes stacked as high as Sabine was tall.

"Seriously, Ming." She walked around him toward the closet. It was packed with men's clothes.

Men's clothes.

"Is this your bedroom?" Sabine asked. She had thought it was a spare room.

"Are you surprised?" Ming picked up a piece of clothing so quickly that Sabine didn't see what it was. He dumped it into a laundry hamper in a corner.

"Just asking. No reason at all."

"My sister and I have lived here for five-plus years, until she married a couple of weeks ago." Ming kicked the pair of flip-flops toward his closet.

"Between the two of us we kept the house nice and clean, but I'm injured at the moment."

"No need to explain anything. I'm more interested in how we can stage the house for sale. If you like, I'll call a maid service for you, but it's not necessary, considering we're going to take everything out of here to begin with."

"Empty out my house?"

"How else are we going to refinish the carpet and paint the walls? Both of us can hardly fit into this room standing up, let alone my crew of four."

"Seems like a lot of work. How much is this going to cost me? I don't have a lot of cash to throw around."

"We'll work on the budget after this tour, okay?" Sabine tapped the wall. The wood was solid. "We'll want to paint the walls a brighter color too."

"I don't care as long as it's not pink." Ming followed her to the bathroom.

This was the smallest closet bathroom Sabine had ever seen. There was a sink, a toilet, and a shower. That was all. Sabine pointed to the popcorn ceiling. It had been everywhere in the house, so she wasn't surprised it was also here.

"First thing I'd do is to get rid of the cabinet under this sink and replace it with a pedestal sink. It'll make the bathroom look bigger."

Sabine turned around, and there was Ming

again. "You know what, Ming? You don't have to tail me. I'm not going to do anything to your house until we've discussed options and worked out a budget."

"Well, I feel like you're invading my privacy."

"Wait until the open house."

"I don't want anybody going through my stuff, especially my personal things."

Sabine laughed. "Most people don't go through a homeowner's things. They just want to see if the house is right for them."

Ming didn't seem convinced.

"If it makes you feel better about it, you can box up your personal stuff until the house sells." Sabine walked around Ming again, but they bumped shoulders at the door.

Ming stepped back. "Sorry. I forgot my manners. After you, ma'am."

Sabine stepped out into the hallway. *Yep. Those brown wall panels have got to go.*

"How long do you think it'll take us to stage this house?" Ming asked. "I hate to say this, but I kinda need the money. I don't want to get on disability, because it means I can't work, but I can't work too much because—why am I telling you all this?"

"Because I'm your agent and you want me to sell this house for half a million dollars."

"Can you sell it for that much?"

"I don't know, but this area is on the up and up. There's potential."

"Good to hear." Ming seemed relieved. "I thought that God wanted me to buy this house."

"He might have for a season. He works that way sometimes. We almost always have to factor in the seasons of our lives."

"Seasons."

Sabine nodded. "A time to buy, a time to sell. A time to stay, a time to leave."

Ming looked pensive.

"Don't feel bad, Ming. There'll always be another house."

"Not this one though. I guess I shouldn't be attached to this house. This world is not my home, as they say."

Sabine wasn't sure what to say to make Ming feel better. This type of beachfront property had higher taxes than the rest of Tybee Island. He had a lot of mortgage left on this house.

"I'm trying to sell my company to your sister, as you know," Ming said.

"I didn't know that." Sabine tried not to feel offended, and truly, there was no reason for her to be. "I'm not privy to my sister's business."

"You and Helen are not close, are you?"

Sabine didn't want to go there. "I'm here to talk about selling this cute little house."

In the living room, Sabine felt that there were too many furniture pieces lying about. She walked through the living room toward the sliding glass door leading outside. "You have a to-die-for view of the ocean and, well, dunes."

"Dunes that block the ocean view."

"For a conservationist, the dunes would be a plus. They're protected by law."

"I like *my* dunes, even though they do take away the view some. You have to be outside to see the ocean."

"That's why you stay outdoors a lot. We can use that to our advantage. Make the deck a part of the livable space in the house."

"I do already. Love my hammock. You think the hammock will sell this house?"

It would take more than that, but Sabine tried to remain optimistic for Ming's sake. "You can hear the waves, and that might be enough for some homeowners."

She fished for her iPhone. No messages. It meant she was free the rest of the day. It was only four o'clock in the afternoon. "Let me take some photos, and then I'll be out of your hair."

"Photos?" Ming looked alarmed. "I haven't cleaned up the house."

"No need. They're just for me to work with. If I had a team of designers, then my team would look at them, but I'm the only designer at my company at this time."

"And me. I'll help. I've got a good eye for things."

Sabine raised an eyebrow.

"You don't believe me?" Ming waved his hands. "See that side table? All wood. I found it at a thrift shop on St. Simon's Island. And that mirror there? You like teal? My sister thought I did great. How much do you think I spent on it? Let me give you a clue: yard sale."

Sabine smiled.

"Come on, Sabine. Guess."

"Okay. Five dollars."

Ming groaned. "How did you know?"

"I didn't. You told me to guess. I was going to start with five and go up from there." Sabine started taking photos. The afternoon sun was in the front of the house, and there really wasn't enough lighting. Before the open house day came, she would call in a photographer friend to take some *after* photos.

Ming's phone buzzed, and he had to take the call. Clicking away on her iPhone, Sabine snapped quick pictures everywhere. When Ming didn't move, Sabine took photos with him in them.

She went through the kitchen to the deck. She stepped off the covered deck into the sun, squinted, and put on her sunglasses. It was only February, and not too hot yet, but the glare of the sun was bright nonetheless. This was the South, after all. Sunny year round.

Sabine walked toward a storage shed by the side of the house. It was old and patched up, but it looked useable. There was a padlock on the door. She stood back and took a picture. Ming came down the low deck toward her.

"Have you ever thought about adding a third bedroom?" Sabine asked.

"Why?"

In the sun, Ming looked almost dashing. Something about his eyes.

Sabine lifted her sunglasses above her head. Oh. His eyes were brown in the sun. They had been dark inside his house. In the sunlight, Ming's black hair had tinges of rusty-colored strands. Sabine did everything she could to not reach out and rub those strands between her fingers.

He's a client!

"It would cost me a fortune to add a third bedroom. Are you recommending I take out a loan?" Ming sighed. "I owe too much, as it is."

"This is a very small house," Sabine explained. "Cozy for one or two people, but if it had three bedrooms, the number of prospective buyers would grow exponentially. Families want more space."

"Three bedrooms will do it?"

"Yep."

"And you're thinking the third bedroom could be where my storage shed is."

"On top of the bedroom, we could have a rooftop deck."

"A rooftop deck, huh?"

"Pine should do it. And a rooftop garden."

"A rooftop garden on a rooftop deck. Sounds luxurious." Ming looked like his stitches were about to burst again.

Wonder why?

Sabine smiled. "It'll all be lovely."

"Yep. A lovely hole in my bank account."

"Behind that wall is your bedroom, isn't it?" Sabine walked toward the window and peered inside. Sure enough. "You could add a long room from here to the front of the house. Your new master suite with a direct view of the ocean."

Ming's frown deepened. "That's a lot of reno. How much is it all going to cost?"

Sabine walked back up the deck, kicking sand off her sandals. "We're going to put all the options on the table and discuss where to go from here. When are you free this week?"

"Well...I have some work I need to do for your sister, so I have no idea."

Sabine scrolled through her calendar. "How

about we set a tentative time? If you can't make it, we'll reschedule."

"Sounds like a plan."

They compared their calendars. Sabine's was filled to the brim with house showings, meetings, closings, and personal stuff, such as taking her mother to the hairdresser's.

Ming's was empty, but he seemed to have saved the entire week for Helen.

For Helen.

Life had to revolve around Helen. Always.

Sabine tried not to take it personally. She focused on her calendar. "How about Wednesday morning? I have an hour open at eleven."

"Why don't we do Friday afternoon and then drive together to Helen's party?" Ming asked.

"You know, I'm tired of her parties. And that's the truth."

"Yet you don't have a choice."

"No." Sabine couldn't say more.

"You have to keep an eye on Mama Hu."

"I don't have a problem staying with Mom and making sure she's okay, but I'm not a party person."

"I know. You hid behind the potted plant last Friday."

"I did not." Sabine knew Ming was teasing, but she didn't like it.

"Next to the pillar you were hugging was a potted plant."

"I wasn't—whatever. I don't care. Where did you get all these ideas about me—oh, Helen." It was just like her sister to go tell everyone about their family. "What did she tell you about our family?"

"All about Mama Hu. And all about you."

"All about me? This I have to hear, but not today." Sabine fished for her car key. She had nowhere to go but home, but she wasn't going to tell him that.

"You seem indifferent." Ming stood in front of her.

He was taller when they were toe to toe. She was wearing a pair of flat sandals today, unlike the heels she'd worn to the Friday night party. Now his lips were at Sabine's eye level, and that was a bad height for his lips to be. She stepped back to clear her mind. She couldn't remember what he had said to her.

"I would think you'd want to know what your sister says about you," Ming continued.

"She says many things."

"She talked nonstop when we were stuck together—undercover, you understand—last week."

"Was that when you hurt yourself again?" Sabine pointed to Ming's stomach.

"I didn't hurt myself. It was a bar fight."

"You were in a bar? I thought you don't drink. That much I know about you from the last party."

"I don't. I had water all night. We were observing someone." Ming grinned, for some reason.

Sabine couldn't read him.

"See, I know you're curious," he said.

"I don't care. What you do with your liver is your business."

"Ha! You're a bit like your sister."

"I'm not anything like my sister," Sabine protested.

"Same family."

"That's all we have in common." And Sabine had less and less in common with Helen for the last three years since—

Don't bring it up.

Forgive, forgive, forgive.

CHAPTER TEN

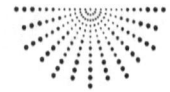

*L*ate Wednesday morning couldn't come soon enough for Ming. He wanted to see Sabine again, regardless of what she would say about the cost of staging his house for sale.

He wanted to see her office, where she worked, how she ran her business outside of Mama Hu's jurisdiction. Standing on her own earned her respect from him, not that it mattered, since she didn't seem to notice his increased interest in her.

She could be pretending to ignore me.

Ming parked several blocks away and walked along East Bay Street toward Sabine's office.

When he entered the office building, he could see the Savannah City Hall a few blocks away and across the street. Up five floors, and Ming found himself ushered into a meeting room with a big wall-mounted television. Sabine's assistant offered him a bottled water.

She left him there for at least fifty minutes.

Ming tried not to be upset about it. He checked his email, sorted out some personal stuff, and read the online news. He threw out the empty water bottle.

A knock on the conference room door made him look up.

"I'm sorry. Miss Hu is still held up." Sabine's assistant was stoic. "Would you like her associate to go over the possible options with you?"

"No. I want Sabine—I mean, I'd rather talk to Sabine because she toured my house, and we've started discussing plans." Ming cleared his throat.

"Very well. Would you like another bottled water?"

"No, thanks."

For some reason, Ming started to worry.

Lord, don't let anything happen to her.

Ming's imagination ran wild. What if her old injuries came back, her legs gave out, and she was in a wreck? What if—

The door flung open.

"Sabine! What happened to you?" Ming exploded out of the chair, and it fell back onto the carpet. He dashed toward Sabine. She had a butterfly tape on her forehead. Her arms were scraped.

"I'm all right. Sorry I'm late." Sabine went for the fallen chair.

Ming stopped her. "Talk to me."

"Why? Are you my big brother now?"

"I'll find out sooner or later. I'll ask Mama Hu if I have to."

"Go ahead." Sabine sat down.

Ming picked up the chair himself. "I want to make sure it doesn't have anything to do with the case Helen and I are working on."

Sabine did not reply. She turned on her laptop and connected it to the big screen. "Do you want to see some options for your house now? Or do you have to go?"

"I have all afternoon." Ming eyed her. "Sooner or later you're going to tell me."

"Tell you what?"

"How you got those bruises."

Sabine folded her arms. "Don't worry about me."

"How can I not? I'm afraid Helen and I are dragging everyone into this mess."

"I don't know what you're talking about."

"The perp that got out on bail. The one who disappeared. The one the Feds are looking for. That one. He's been harassing some of Helen's employees."

"I don't work for Helen."

"But you're her sister."

She looked so calm that Ming believed she was okay. Still, it bothered him that she hadn't said how she was bruised. "Sabine, look at me."

Sabine didn't.

He sat down on the chair next to her. His shoulders sagged when he saw her eyes. She had been crying at some point this morning.

"What happened?"

Sabine forced a smile. "We're running late. We need to get started so we can budget the—"

"I don't have to get to church until seven o'clock this evening. I can wait patiently until you talk to me. You don't have a meeting this afternoon, do you?"

He did not expect Sabine to lie to him. She didn't say a word.

"That looks fresh." Ming's finger touched her hairline where the butterfly tape was. "Someone attacked you this morning. I can always find out from SCMPD what happened."

"Go ahead."

"But I'd rather hear it from you."

"I have nothing to tell you."

"Let me be the judge of that." Ming held Sabine's hand.

Sabine drew a deep breath. "Okay. I was coming out of Mom's house, walking to my SUV. She has overnight guests, and they took up all the parking in her garage. I had to park at the curb. While I was looking for my keys, someone came up from behind me and knocked me down."

"Go on."

"It was in broad daylight. Some tourists shouted at him, and he ran. I filed a police report." Sabine let go of Ming's hand. "That's all."

"How did you get that cut on your forehead?"

"Oh that. When he knocked me down, I fought back."

That's my girl.

Ming knew there was a fighter in Sabine.

"And he pushed me onto a metal trash can holder. Good thing my tetanus shot is up to date."

"You don't smell like trash." Ming laughed.

"Ha-ha. Clever. I went home and took a shower before I came here."

"Well, I'm glad you're safe." Ming wondered if there was more to it than what she had said, but Sabine looked tired. "May I pray?"

"With me?"

Ming nodded. When she didn't protest, Ming closed his eyes. "Father God, thank You for keeping

Sabine safe this morning. Continue to keep us safe, and please catch the mugger. In Jesus' Name I pray. Amen."

It was a simple prayer, but Ming meant every word.

"Thank you. Are you ready to talk about your house?" Sabine logged into her laptop.

"I need to know how much the reno will cost." Ming's stomach rumbled.

"Have you eaten lunch?" Sabine asked.

"Ah, no."

"Oh. I made you wait in my office."

"You didn't make me wait. Your assistant asked me if I wanted to reschedule, and I said no. I waited of my own volition."

"Why don't you order something from the café downstairs? They'll bring it up." Sabine gave Ming the website address. Ming checked the menu. The items were pretty reasonably priced. He ordered a panini sandwich and soda.

When he turned off his iPhone, he found Sabine staring at him. "What?"

"Nothing."

Nothing, huh? Ming tried to read Sabine's face, but couldn't see a thing.

CHAPTER ELEVEN

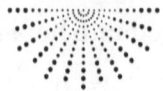

"*T*hat wasn't so painful, was it?" Sabine asked as she backed the SUV out of the parking spot.

"No. I was surprised." Ming fastened his seat belt on the passenger side. "Whew. I thought it was going to cost a fortune."

"Painting is almost always the cheapest way to pretty up a house for sale. I wish, though, that we could've added the master suite I suggested, but that's the way it goes." In fact, Sabine thought that if she had extra cash, she could buy Ming's house and turn it into a rental. But she had prayed about it, and didn't think that was the direction she should take.

Sell it and move on.

"I like the idea, and I want it, but my piggy bank is lean and mean these days."

"I hear you. I'm impressed you didn't let me talk you into it." Sabine locked her doors as she turned onto East Bay Street and headed for the warehouses in Richmond on the other side of Savannah.

Ming shrugged. "I'm just picking up a few tips from my brother-in-law. He operates everything debt-free."

"Good for him and your sister."

"Like you said, we'll suggest expansion possibilities to the prospective buyers."

"It'll make the side yards smaller, but hey, there's a whole beach in the backyard."

Ming nodded.

"You'll love these warehouses. I've found some nice dining sets at reasonable prices." Sabine hoped to get some good finds for Ming's house. It would work out, and the budget was reasonable for him. It helped that she had given him a labor discount in exchange for using his house as a show home for the interior decorating side of her company.

The dashboard clock said it was almost two. They had a few hours left before Ming had to leave. He had invited her to church with him tonight, but she had turned him down. After this morning, all she wanted to do was go home and soak in her outdoor hot tub.

Get all that pain out.

Sabine's phone rang. She had to take the call to

line up some house showings. When she hung up, she turned on the radio. Ming didn't say anything. He seemed to be texting.

When he was done, he took a deep breath.

"Everything okay?" Sabine asked above the classical music that filled the SUV.

Ming didn't nod. One of his hands fisted up. "Yeah. Fine."

Sabine didn't ask further because she didn't want to pry—

The school bus came out of nowhere.

Sabine slammed on her brakes. She could hear the wheels screech. She jerked the steering wheel to the right and came to a complete stop in the emergency lane.

Ahead, the school bus went its merry way.

Sabine buried her face in her hands.

"Whoa." Ming's voice was loud in Sabine's ears. "What was that?"

"I thought the school bus...well, it...I don't know."

"Let me drive, Sabine."

"I just need a minute."

Ming put his hand on Sabine's arm. "Let me drive."

After a bit, she nodded. She left the key in the ignition, unfastened her seat belt, and carefully got out of her SUV. She felt relieved that Ming had offered to drive.

She slid into the passenger seat.

She wasn't sure what had overcome her.

It was as if all her senses had been heightened by what had happened that morning.

It had been an unusual mugging. Savannah wasn't that kind of place. They should be able to walk about in daylight. She was leaving her sister's house after dealing with yet another hangover morning pity party her mom had, when she was accosted from behind and pushed to the sidewalk.

If not for some tourists shouting at the mugger, Sabine would've been badly hurt.

The whole event probably had nothing to do with whatever Helen was working on.

Or it could have everything to do with Helen's high-profile work.

I'm just the no-name sister. Leave me alone!

Ming got them on the road in no time. He drove with one hand. The other hand was holding Sabine's. He didn't let go, and Sabine didn't protest.

"I'm taking you home." He made a U-turn.

Sabine didn't know what to say.

"I'm dropping you off. You don't have to invite me inside."

"I live alone. Mom sometimes show up, but I rarely have visitors."

"I live alone too, and you showed up at my house."

"I'm selling your house. It's business."

"This is business too. If you were mugged because of the case that Helen and I are working on, I would be ticked off." Ming practically growled. "We'll have to find a way to protect you."

"The only way is for you to put me in God's hands."

"Well, I'll pray about that too," Ming said. "Okay, we're heading into Savannah. Need to know where I should take you, or we'll be driving around in circles."

Sabine gave him the directions.

"Now, that wasn't so hard, was it?" Ming asked.

"I feel like you would be invading my privacy if you knew where I live. And how are you going to get your car that is parked at my office?"

"I'll call a cab or Uber or Lyft. Don't worry, Sabine. It's not like I'm going to go to your bedroom to tuck you in. I'll even sit outside at the curb to wait to be picked up if it gives you more privacy."

Sabine was sure he meant it. "Yet here we are, holding hands."

Ming grinned.

"Meaning what, exactly?" Sabine asked.

"What? I just grinned."

"Uh-huh."

"I would love to see where you live and know what kind of life you lead though."

"Another time." Sabine sighed.

"Right. I do know you're low key."

"That's me. A backstage type of person. Unlike my sister."

"I know so little about you, only what Helen says."

Sabine turned away. "Helen has her own lenses."

"You two seem to get along."

"For Mom's sake, we have to."

"Otherwise?"

Sabine didn't like Ming's prying. "Otherwise what? We're sisters. We try to avoid each other as much as possible, but when it comes to family, all differences have to be put aside for unity."

"Or a united front?"

"Is it your business, Ming?"

"I suppose not."

They drove in silence the rest of the way.

CHAPTER TWELVE

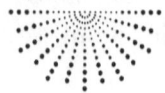

"Where are you?" Ming's voice came through clearly on Sabine's phone. "I hear people."

"Belford's. Mom's date night." Sabine leaned back in her chair two tables away from Mom's. It was her turn tonight to drive Mom, and she decided she might as well stay and have dinner. Alone.

"Babysitting Mama Hu."

"Not exactly. Mom doesn't want to look for a parking spot, and she didn't want her date to pick her up. I dropped her off. You know, curbside service and all."

"And you're the designated driver."

"I got free dinner out of it."

"At least you're not sitting and eating in your car."

"Are you?" Sabine asked.

A long sigh came through. "Not in my own car, but I'm done though. For the night."

"So whatcha doing now?" Sabine asked.

"Driving home."

"Get some rest, okay? Let the wounds heal." It was good to hear from him, though it had only been two days. How could anyone miss an acquaintance in two days? "If you don't move around too much, the stitches won't go stretching this way and that."

"We have a lot in common." His voice was quiet, perhaps even contemplative.

Sabine didn't know how to respond. She decided to keep it impersonal. "Injuries require time to heal."

"Encouragement helps."

"And prayers. God answers prayers."

"Amen," Ming said. "So what are you doing besides eating? Just sitting there, waiting?"

"Something like that. I'm planning my schedule. Trying to get your house ready for an open house. Does the twelfth sound good to you?"

"March?"

"Uh-huh. April would be too far away. We can get the reno done in two weeks since you picked the easiest, minimalist staging option."

"Sabine."

"Yes, Ming?"

"Don't you think of anything else besides work?"

Sabine shrugged. "I'll read a book in a minute, but I've had a long week."

"It's only Thursday."

"Almost Friday."

"What do you do on weekends?"

"Isn't that a personal question? Do you ask that of your business associates?" Sabine nodded as the server placed her arugula salad in front of her. It looked delicious.

"Business associates? Is that all we are?" Ming sounded hurt.

"I'm your real estate agent. You're my client."

"Prior to this, we knew each other."

"But we didn't have this much interaction." Sabine paused. "About last Friday..."

"Nothing happened last Friday. We didn't even follow through with our dance."

"You doubled over in great pain."

"I did not."

"Look, Ming. I'd love to chat with you, but my salad just arrived."

"Your salad. So you're not done eating? It's almost seven thirty."

"Mom's date had to work until six o'clock, and traffic held him up until minutes ago."

Sabine glanced over to find Mom deep in

conversation with her date. He had a bushy red beard and an untrimmed mustache covering half his face, so Sabine couldn't tell if he was smiling or frowning.

Mom's hand was all over his arm.

Well, looks like Mom's moving on from the two Leungs.

For Sabine, she preferred clean-shaven faces.

Like Ming's.

"I'll let you go," Ming said.

Don't let me go.

"All right. See you tomorrow maybe?"

"I'll be working in the middle of the night through lunch, then I'm going home to crash. By then painters would be done, right?"

"I hope so, for your sake. I'm not sure if it's good for anyone's lungs to sleep in paint fumes."

Ming said nothing.

"Hello?" Sabine said. "Did I just lose you?"

"You didn't lose me. I was thinking about how thoughtful you are."

"Paint fumes, Ming. Anybody would think of that."

"I guess so. I'll sleep on my hammock. Or move my cot to the deck."

"Well, they're going to restain the deck tomorrow afternoon."

"I'll sleep in my car."

"You're silly." Sabine laughed.

"Am I?"

This time, Ming's voice was louder, filled her other ear, and didn't sound like it came from her iPhone.

She froze. Then turned.

Ming was standing right next to her table, wearing an unzipped hooded jacket. Inside was a dark tee shirt to match. Ming always looked good regardless of what he wore. His jeans were tight and his legs long, making the table look low.

Sabine's iPhone slid off her ear.

CHAPTER THIRTEEN

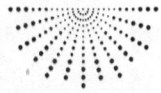

"*I*s this seat taken?" Ming pointed to the empty chair across from Sabine.

"Uh, no." Sabine looked happy to see him, but he couldn't tell. "How did you know where to find us?"

"This is Mama Hu's favorite restaurant in Savannah."

"And you have her schedule."

"I asked Helen." Ming smiled. "Your forehead looks pretty good."

"Scab should form soon." Sabine gently touched the butterfly tape with her finger. "Won't you sit down?"

"Thank you." Ming found his knees almost reaching hers beneath the table. *Too close.*

He pushed the salon chair back and away from the exposed brick wall that was one of the signature designs of Belford's.

"I love everything here." A server came to give him the menu. He asked for a glass of water with lime in it.

All this time, Sabine stared at him.

"Feel free to eat your salad," Ming said.

"I'll wait for you to order."

"I've already had some cold pizza. But I might get a bowl of soup. Have you said grace?"

"Not yet."

"Would you like me to say it for both of us?" Ming asked.

"Sure. Feel free."

Feel free? What did she mean by that?

Ming reached across the table and held Sabine's hand. She didn't withdraw it, so that was a good sign. Problem was, he didn't know why he was so forward, as if he were in a hurry, which he really shouldn't be.

Sabine had some emotional healing to deal with from that wreck that had nearly taken her life.

Well, maybe that was why he was here. Maybe God had put him here to be with her.

Ming closed his eyes and said the quickest blessing ever. "I'm sorry. I'll do better next time."

"That's all right. You should hear Mom say a blessing."

"Never heard her say it."

"Exactly."

"It could be legalistic to expect a Christian to say a blessing before we eat every time. Sometimes we forget. It's not like we're going to lose our salvation because we forget to thank God for the food He has provided for us."

"I know." She said nothing more.

"Please eat. My soup will be here shortly."

"Uh-huh. You haven't even ordered it."

The server came quickly enough, and Ming did order his soup. He watched Sabine eat. He tried to ascertain if she was nervous that he had invited himself to dinner with her.

"How did you get here so fast?" Sabine asked.

"I told you. I was on my way home."

"You didn't say from where."

"We—me and you-know-who—were in the area."

"That's all you can say."

"That's all I can say." Ming wanted to tell her more, but she had no business knowing. It was a job, and he was getting paid for it, and that was all that mattered. It was an easy job, sitting in the van gabbing with Helen all day long. Besides, when Helen talked, she talked.

One of these days, he'd ask her all about Sabine.

Then again, why not ask Sabine herself?

Ming's she-crab soup came, looking delicious. He was surprised he was suddenly hungry again. Belford's did that to him every time. He'd drive here thinking he'd have a half sandwich, and then drive home having eaten a steak.

"That looks good," Sabine said.

"Want some?" There he went again. Before he could think, he was lifting a spoon in the air toward Sabine.

She hesitated.

And hesitated.

"The spoon is clean," Ming said.

"Okay." Sabine leaned forward, chuckling. "This is silly."

Ming couldn't believe he fed her a spoonful of soup. He handed the spoon to Sabine. "Keep the spoon."

Sabine didn't look offended at all. "Exactly what I would've done. My kind of g—oops."

"Guy? Your kind of guy?" From the corner of Ming's eye he spotted Helen's associate sitting at a far corner table facing in their direction.

Earl nodded ever so slightly to him.

Ming felt only a tad better that Helen had dispatched Earl to follow Mama Hu and Sabine around. He wanted Helen to assign a permanent bodyguard for Sabine. But Helen didn't think it was necessary.

It was up to Ming now.

As long as their fugitive didn't get near Sabine, Ming felt that she was safe.

Two tables away, Mama Hu's hands were all over her date.

"Mama Hu's having fun." Ming kept his voice low. "That doesn't look like Leung."

"She has moved on," Sabine said. "Give her some privacy, will you?"

"Since when did she go cougar?" Ming could tell that the bearded man was considerably younger than Mama Hu.

"It's not like that." Sabine bristled.

"No? Last three guys she has dated have all been half her age." Ming flagged down the server to get a new spoon.

"You pried?"

"Helen."

"I should've known. She talks too much." Sabine sighed.

"I'm sorry. Let's talk about something else." Ming chided himself for bringing up Helen. He could tell she was somewhat of a sore point for Sabine, though they were sisters and all. He could understand that a little bit. When he had tiffs with his own sister, it wasn't pretty.

But they always made up.

Only here, he could sense that there was something unresolved between Sabine and her sister.

"I don't know what we can talk about," Sabine said as her entrée arrived.

"Is that cod?"

"Halibut." Sabine dug in. "Delicious. Want some?"

"Uh, sure."

"Don't be coy. You practically tried to feed me earlier."

"I didn't try. I succeeded."

Sabine rotated her dinner plate. "Here. Try some. Use your own fork."

"We have our own dinner etiquette, you mean?" Ming laughed, then gripped his stomach.

Sabine made a sound. "Sorry. Poor thing, you."

"I'll heal. Soon enough." He reached over with his fork. The halibut was delicious. "They don't usually serve halibut."

"Tonight's special."

"Indeed it is." Ming thought the light eyeliner on Sabine's eyes was becoming on her. She had pulled her hair up into a ponytail.

There was that necklace again. Gold cross on a gold chain. He wanted to ask her who had bought it for her, but that would put him in the busybody category, and perhaps even turn her off.

Sabine must've noticed where his eyes had gone. She lifted the cross. "My dad gave this to me."

Ah, her dad. A lot of memories there. "So sorry about your dad."

"God's timing and all."

Ming nodded. "Life is hard."

"Heaven's fun for him. No more worries. No more running after Helen and me, making sure we—"

Silence.

"Go on." Ming scooped up the last bit of his soup.

Sabine hesitated.

"I'm your buddy, remember?" Ming said.

"Well, okay. Dad was always making sure we dated the right guys. He didn't want the family name tainted by riffraffs, as he called it. I mean, not that we'd—"

Ming smiled. "I get the idea, though I'm not exactly sure what you were trying to say if you don't finish your sentences. I'll try to guess the rest of your thoughts, but if I fail miserably, it'll be your fault."

That broke the ice. Sabine relaxed a bit, or so Ming thought.

"Want more halibut?" she asked. "I'm not too hungry tonight."

"Sure. Give me half." Ming asked the server for a plate. "My sister's favorite food is the salmon burger that I grill. To perfection, I might add. Maybe someday, I could—we could—"

Am I being too forward?

"I'll try to guess the rest of that sentence, but if I fail miserably, it'll be your fault." Sabine pointed at him.

"Ha-ha." Ming divided Sabine's halibut into two pieces.

"When we sell your house, you owe me a salmon burger," Sabine said.

"Deal. And we'll celebrate with my sister and Diego."

"Your sister is very important to you, isn't she?"

"Yes. What she says is very important to me. Her opinion about everything matters to me."

"Is that why you want me to meet her?"

Busted! Ming didn't know how to respond. Yes, he wanted Heidi's impression of Sabine. If Heidi didn't like her, then he couldn't possibly...

Couldn't possibly what?

Go out with her?

We're having dinner now, aren't we, even though I invited myself?

"What do you usually do on weekends?" The question rolled out of Ming's mouth as if he had no control over it. In his heart, he wanted to spend more time with Sabine, but he felt he might be rushing it.

"This weekend I'll be working on your house. They're painting tomorrow and should be done by Saturday. I don't want them to work on Sundays. They'll go back there on Monday."

"You're sure they'll be done in two weeks?"

"They'd better be before the open house." Sabine produced her iPhone from her purse. "You sure you don't want to go shopping with me?"

"I want to, but I can't. I'm committed to this project with Helen, and I get paid if I finish the work."

"You sure you're letting me pick out whatever furniture I want for your house?"

"Just make sure it's within budget. Besides, it won't be my house much longer." Ming felt sad. It had been his house for five years. His and Heidi's. Heidi had married and moved out, but there were memories in the house.

"You wish you could keep the house."

How did Sabine read him this well? Ming nodded. "Maybe even rent it out... Nah. Better sell it."

"Well, if you can rent it out, the income could offset your monthly payments."

"You think there's potential." Ming folded his arms. The server took his bowl away. And the empty plate with zero bits of halibut left.

"Sure. You have a cute house by the sea. It's

built well, has a great view—an even better one once we build that rooftop deck. You could rent it out all year. It might not bring in too much profit as a vacation rental, but a family with kids would love the space."

A family with kids.

"Don't you have any feelings of nostalgia, ever, for what once was?" Ming asked.

"I sell houses, not memories."

"The past is not always painful, Sabine."

"I'd rather keep moving ahead."

"Wasn't there anything good out of your past that you might want to cherish?" Ming reached across the table.

"Since Dad died, many things have happened to us. A lot of bad things."

"Unhappy things."

Sabine looked like she was nodding, then held herself back. Ming saw it though, that slight nod. He felt that she didn't want to show her feelings.

"God can make all things new. I read that in the Bible." He tried to assure her.

"Yes, and looking forward is the best way to keep things fresh and new."

"You didn't hear me, Sabine. God is the One who can make all things new. We can't. He can."

"He's already healed me, Ming."

"Physically, yes. But emotionally?"

Sabine didn't answer.

"We may not see it right now, but God is continuing His good work in you and me."

"Says Buddy Ming?" Sabine asked.

Buddy.

Is that all you think of me?

CHAPTER FOURTEEN

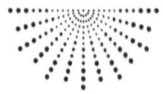

"No, Albert. You're not going to get better *sitting a spell*." Sabine tried not to pace up and down Ming's stripped-down deck. The canvas awning had been removed so the painters could paint the outside walls.

One of her interior design employees was in pain. Clearly in pain. The kind of pain Sabine had known when her legs were broken in that wreck on Interstate 95 three years before. Yeah, the one that nearly killed her.

But Albert had refused any help. He'd been sitting in that folding chair the whole time Sabine had tried to reason with him.

No more than forty minutes before, her team leader had called her after Albert had fallen off a scaffolding while scraping popcorn off Ming's ceiling. The moment Sabine had received the call, she abandoned her breakfast and was in her SUV before she hung up the phone.

Twenty minutes of speeding to Tybee Island later, the sun had barely risen over the Atlantic. The swooshing, ebbing tide had cleansed the shoreline. This would be a good time for a beach stroll, coffee in hand.

But nope. She had to stare down at Albert. Good old Albert. One of her oldest painters, and more stubborn than Mom.

"Let a doc look at that, Albert," one of the other painters said. The others chimed in, echoing the encouragement.

"I can't max out the deductibles." Albert moaned. "The wife needs it for her treatment."

"Albert." Sabine took a deep breath. "Look at me."

Albert didn't.

"I'll pay for it. You need that arm looked at. If it's broken—"

"It's not broken!"

"How do you know? Have you gone to medical school? The last thing you'd want is for your dear wife to worry, right? Do you want me to call her to come out here and drive you to the doc?"

Albert put his good hand up. "Okay, okay. I'll go. You don't have to pay for it."

"I insist."

"No, Miss Sabine. No need." Albert tried to get up. His coworkers helped him.

"Let's get him to my vehicle," Sabine said. "I'll drive."

"Joey can drive," Albert said feebly and pointed to one of Sabine's new hires.

"No can do, Albert. I've got a feeling Joey is going to drive you home instead. I'm taking you straight to the walk-in clinic, and you're going to stay there until we hear what the doctor has to say."

Nobody said a word. No one dared to counter Sabine.

"She's stubborn like that."

Helen?

Sabine spun around. There she was. Her sister standing petite and very pretty next to Ming— Ming!—who was staring at her.

Oh no. Sabine realized she was wearing—

"You're in shorts," Helen said.

It was loud enough for everyone to hear.

"I'm glad you're wearing shorts outside the house now," Helen continued. "It gets old seeing you in pants and long skirts in public all the time."

Sabine couldn't speak. Ming was still staring at her. Now he was looking at her legs.

Her legs!

Her scarred, stitched up, ugly legs, with pins and rods and three years of therapy.

Oh, she wished she had slipped on a pair of pants before she left the house.

Sabine felt like running inside and hiding in the bathroom. But she couldn't. She had to take Albert to the clinic. She had to step off the deck and walk past Ming to the side yard to get to her SUV parked out front.

Her legs became jello.

Ming leapt up the deck two or three steps at a time and was by her side, one hand on her arm.

Sabine straightened up. "I'm okay. I think I tripped."

"You were standing still. Then you went wobbly." Ming's voice was almost a whisper. "You didn't trip."

"I need to go." She motioned for her workers to get Albert going. "I'm taking Albert to the doc, and y'all will keep painting, okay?"

They all agreed.

"I can help," Ming said. "I can drive."

"Not necessary, Ming." Sabine smiled.

Helen was still standing in the yard at the foot of the pine steps. "Did you forget something, Ming? You have to go pick up your sister from the airport."

"Oh yeah." Ming checked his watch. "That's right."

"And you need a couple of hours of sleep, or you can't drive." Helen would have kept talking had her phone not buzzed.

Ming grinned at Sabine. "Your sister likes to order people around."

Sabine did not respond to that.

"I have to go." She picked up her pace. She could hear her SUV doors opening and closing out front. "See you later. I'll make sure they finish painting today, okay?"

Ming went after her. In the side yard, his long strides matched hers. "Sabine."

"What?" Sabine turned just as Ming's fingers touched her arm.

His other hand was gentle on her shoulder. That grin still plastered on his face, his lips met hers. Ming's show of affection warmed Sabine from lips to her fingertips.

What does this mean?

What about my scars?

Sabine's eyelids were half-closed. "Why are you doing this?"

"Why not?" Ming's voice was low and oh so soothing. He leaned in for another kiss.

Don't stop—

Reality hit her. "My guy is in pain, sitting in the SUV, waiting for me to take him to the only open clinic I can think of, save for the ER. Have a care, will you?"

Sabine was surprised at what came out of her mouth. She could've at least enjoyed the moment, she chided herself.

I do, but—

"Just one sec." Ming tried to kiss her again.

This time she pulled away. "Must go!"

Sabine ran.

CHAPTER FIFTEEN

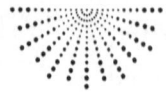

"Glad you were bumped up to first class," Ming said to his new brother-in-law as he drove away from the Savannah/Hilton Head International Airport.

It had taken him fifty minutes in light traffic to drive from his house on Tybee Island to the airport, and then he sat at baggage claim for forty minutes, wishing he had slept an extra thirty minutes at home. It was good for everyone that the flight from Kennedy had arrived on time.

"Yeah. That was unexpected." Diego Flores looked ahead. In the backseat, Heidi was dozing off, held in place only by her seat belt.

"A nice finish to your honeymoon."

"Yep."

"You look tired, man."

Diego didn't say a word.

Ming knew that in spite of the long flight from Naples to New York by way of Rome, the two newlyweds had stayed overnight in New York City, with a stopover Friday night dinner and rest at a nice hotel, before their morning flight from Kennedy to Savannah.

"How did my dad do?" Diego changed the subject.

"Very well." Ming meant it. Pastor Flores, the senior, had taken good care of the flock while Diego and Heidi were away for three weeks. "He kept saying he missed preaching."

"Well, he'll make a good addition to our church."

Ming nodded. "I think it's a good idea. Some senior members of Riverside don't want to see our church run by young ones."

"Ha. We're not young."

"To them, thirtysomething means inexperienced."

"Well, we have Dad now. They're going to have to put up with him as our new Counseling Pastor. It doesn't matter if they're nine or ninety. He's counseling everyone in everything, from grief to marriage."

"Yeah, I remember your six-week premarital boot camp."

"That's Dad for you." Diego laughed. "So, tell me. What did you do while we were gone? Did you stay out of trouble? Have your scars healed?"

Scars?

Diego's word reminded Ming of Sabine's legs. He could still see her legs.

Some fierce scars there.

He hadn't noticed, until Helen mentioned it, that Sabine had never worn anything shorter than a pair of pants. He had never seen her legs until this morning. If not for that man's injured arm, she would not have shown up at Ming's house dressed in tee shirt and shorts.

Every time they had been together, she had been covered up, but impeccably dressed.

Like the model she used to be.

Helen had told him a bit about that. Sabine had toured the European and Asian circuits for a few years after college. She had been on the up-and-up when she took a two-week vacation to visit her mother. Who would have imagined that a trip to the hair salon with Helen could put Sabine in the hospital for six months?

"You're not answering my question, Ming." Diego tried again. "Something's going on."

"I met someone. Well, I've known her a bit in the past, but we have really met this time."

"Oh?"

"I think it's more than friendship."

"Okay."

"I think I'm moving beyond just liking her."

"And?"

"And I don't intend to wait five years like you did before you told Heidi."

"God's timing, Ming, is not the same for everyone. I waited five years. Maybe you won't wait five months."

Months? I'm thinking days.

"I want to tell her now, but I'm not sure how she's going to take it."

"Someone I know?"

"Not directly. But you know of her sister. Helen Hu?"

"Yes. We pray for your projects with her from time to time. Hu Knows or something."

"Yep. That's the new name of the company. Sabine doesn't work for Helen, but she shows up every now and then at company activities to keep an eye on Mama Hu."

"Sabine, is it?"

"You'll be happy to know I invited Sabine to church, and she went last Sunday."

"Good." Diego paused.

It was a long pause. It made Ming worry. "She's a believer, Diego. Just hasn't found a church home."

"Glad to hear that. Why don't you fill me in so we can talk?"

Ming glanced at the rearview mirror. Heidi was asleep in the backseat.

He wasn't sure he wanted a third opinion about Sabine at this time. "We could talk another time. You had a long flight. I can make an appointment or something."

"Ming! You're my old friend, and now you're my brother-in-law. No formalities necessary."

"Well, I kind of need some counseling on how to proceed."

"I can tell you the first step right now, and we'll flesh out the details later. How's that?" Diego asked.

"Sounds good."

"Before I do anything, make any decision, you know that I always try to find out what God says about it."

"You do. But you take too long."

"You're not me," Diego said. "Each believer in Christ has to seek God's perfect will for our individual circumstances. The only thing that fits everybody's needs all at once is salvation in Jesus Christ. After that comes sanctification. That's a life-long process, and it's custom fit for each believer according to the work of the Holy Spirit and the Word of God."

"Diego, you missed preaching, didn't you?"

Ming laughed as he turned onto a back road toward Diego's apartment to avoid traffic going toward River Street, where it would be crowded near the waterfront area.

"Yeah, I did. All three weeks. I can see now why it's hard for my dad to sit back and let someone else preach."

"Why don't you give him a Sunday School class to teach?"

"That's a great idea, Ming. Wow. I should've thought of that."

"I'll take a cup of coffee as payment for that advice."

"You drive a hard bargain, man." Diego glanced back. "Heidi is still asleep."

"Jet lag."

"Tell you what. Why don't we drop her off, then you and I can go have a cuppa?"

"If you want to."

"For sure. I want to hear all about this lady you're madly in love with."

"Not madly." *Maybe just a little.*

Well, okay. A lot.

CHAPTER SIXTEEN

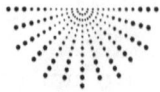

*P*iper's Place was packed at noon on Saturday, but Ming was glad the restaurant had added seating on the third floor, which used to be Piper Peyton's apartment. The view of the Savannah River was glorious this sunny day as Ming ordered breakfast while Diego ordered lunch.

"I can't believe you're selling your house." Diego handed the menu back to the server.

"It's a hole in the ground." Ming stirred cream into his coffee mug.

"You like that place."

"I love my house."

"Love? You've never been this intense over things."

"What do you mean?" Ming's eyebrows rose.

"In all these years we've been buddies, you've never been attached to things. Houses, cars, furniture, properties. Not even your job. You'd sell your company in a heartbeat if the situation looks right."

Buddies?

The word irritated Ming now. At the party the Friday night before, he and Sabine had agreed to be buddies.

He wondered what Sabine thought of their relationship now that he had kissed her. Were they still buddies? Somehow *kissing buddies* didn't sound right to him.

She had responded, hadn't she?

Let him kiss her, hadn't she?

"Hello?" Diego said. "Did I trigger something?"

"Buddies."

"That we are."

"I told Sabine that I wanted us to be buddies."

"Sabine. Ah, the woman you're madly in love with." Diego sat back on his bench seat across from Ming. "Why don't you fill me in so I'm not guessing this and that?"

Ming thought he could do that. Their booth was secluded enough in this corner of the top floor of Piper's Place that nobody would pay any attention to what they were discussing. The probability of someone here at this time knowing Sabine and reporting back to her about his conversation with Diego was miniscule.

Well, more people knew her sister, Helen, and Hu Knows, Inc.

I don't care.

Ming had a problem, and it needed a solution. From all his years of friendship with Diego, Ming knew that Diego would tell him the solution was a spiritual one. Still, if anyone could be objective about his situation, Diego would be. Ming wasn't afraid of his biblical solutions, all those verses Diego had given him over the years, all those *pray to God* reminders his old friend had generously dispensed. He welcomed them.

"Let's hear it," Diego said.

"You're a patient man, my friend." Ming wondered what to say, how much to say, and when to say it.

"Heidi says I'm too patient."

"That too." Ming wondered about himself. He was definitely not as patient as Diego. If he were, he wouldn't have taken that extra job two weeks before and busted his stitches. He'd be sitting at home, waiting for his internal wounds to gel up a bit before he went back to work.

If his sister found out about his impatience,

she'd be mad at him. It was because she cared. Just like Diego. He cared.

Thank You, Lord, for caring friends and family.

"Are you going to tell all this to Heidi?" Ming asked.

"Not if you don't want me to, but I value her input, her insight, and you might want to consider her female perspective."

"Good point. I trust both of you. Okay, you can tell her whatever I tell you here."

"Thank you. Now, you want to talk about the house first or about Sabine?"

"They're both connected. Sabine is the agent selling my house. She's also an interior designer, so she's fixing up my house—she called it staging—to sell. She did have some grand ideas that I can't afford, but we're going to present those to prospective buyers. She's having her general contractor draw up some expansion plans so families might be more interested."

"Expansion? Families?"

"She thinks if my house has more than two bedrooms, it'll attract more buyers."

"If it has a bigger living room..."

"That too. You know the yard on that side? Just grass and bushes. Useless space." *Uh, not true.* He had kissed Sabine there this morning. It would always be their special place. The place of their first kisses.

Ming wished he had picked a more memorable spot.

Well, I had to kiss her.

"So. Sabine is staging and selling your house. You two work together. You fell in love. Did I get that right?" Diego asked.

"Not in that order, necessarily. I've seen her around the last couple of years. She always kept to herself, but I found her intriguing."

"But you were dating other people."

"Do we have to recite the history of my love life?"

"Sabine rose above the crowd of dates."

"Yes, though we haven't actually dated"—Ming made quotation marks in the air with his fingers— "she was at Belford's on Thursday, chaperoning Mama Hu, and I dropped in. We had dinner."

"She didn't mind?"

"She liked my company. Or so it seemed."

Their main courses came. Diego said a blessing, and they dug in.

"What does she think of you?" Diego asked.

"That I'm kind." Ming sprinkled pepper on his scrambled eggs. He looked up. "What? You don't agree?"

Diego pointed to his mouthful of food.

Whatever.

"She has issues," Ming continued.

"So do you."

"Me? I don't have issues, except with work anxieties. I wish my company were more stable. Then I wouldn't have to sell it."

Diego put down his fork. "Ming."

"Yeah? That's my name."

"Ming, old friend. You're selling everything? Your business, your house? What are you going to do? Where are you going to go?"

"I'm moving in with you and Heidi." Ming laughed. But Diego had a point. "I've got to heal from these injuries, man. Business is not going well. I'm afraid of defaulting on my house payments. I don't think I can sustain this."

"Uh-huh."

Uh-oh. That can only mean one thing. "Give it to me, Diego. I can handle it."

"Let's make a list." Diego counted with his fingers. "Health. Job. House. Woman."

"What are you getting at?" Ming finished his breakfast. The server asked him if he wanted another pecan pancake. He said no.

"You have four issues stacked on top of one another."

Ming shook his head. "Sabine is not an issue."

"Everything happening at the same time is."

"You know me. I multitask." Ming drank more coffee. In fact, he could drink a whole carafe of it.

"In order of priorities, number them."

"Sabine comes first."

"Wrong answer, Ming."

"I knew it. I can't even pass a simple test. I'm doomed," Ming joked. "So what good am I?"

"Like useless rags. You know the Bible calls us filthy rags."

"I don't remember that verse." Ming was serious.

Diego swiped his iPhone. "Isaiah 64:6. Here we go."

> But we are all as an unclean thing, and all our righteousnesses are as filthy rags; and we all do fade as a leaf; and our iniquities, like the wind, have taken us away.

"Wow. Okay. Meaning what?"

"Meaning we need God."

"Now, more than ever. I'm in a big mess, Diego."

"No, you're not. You think you are because your problems are piled up. Let's take them apart, prioritize them." Diego produced a pen. He placed a napkin on the table. Scribbled this and that on it. "Four things concern you right now, but there is a fifth, and it should be your first."

"That is?"

"Who, not what." Diego wrote a word on top of the list. Spun the napkin around and pushed it toward Ming.

God.

That was on top of the list. Ming pointed to the napkin. "You didn't number the rest."

"Those items are between you and God. Put God first, and all things become clear."

"I do, Diego. I read my Bible every morning, and I go to church twice every Sunday, and occasionally on Wednesday evenings, if I'm not working."

"Good for you. But those are works. You read. You go. You do. God wants to be the priority in your heart. God wants to be your first love."

"I know that verse. It's in Revelation." Ming's stomach was full, but his heart was downcast. "Does it mean Sabine is not for me?"

"I didn't say that. I say that in order for you to truly love Sabine, you must first love God."

"With all my heart, mind, and soul. I know that. What am I missing?"

"True love comes from God. Out of God's love, you will be able to love Sabine with the purest, unadulterated love. That's God's love at its pinnacle on earth."

"But we have a sin nature."

"Pinned to the cross of Christ. Through His

Spirit, we can now love in the fullest sense of the word."

"Diego, you are wise."

Diego shook his head. "God is wise. I'm just sharing what I've learned."

"Man, you've learned a lot. Tell me more."

CHAPTER SEVENTEEN

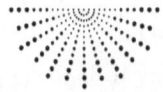

S abine's hair was still wet when she waltzed into Ming's house carrying boxes of hot fried chicken for her crew. They were happy to see her, and even happier to see the free dinner. She inspected the work.

"Nicely done, guys."

The popcorn ceiling was gone. The new smooth ceiling was up. The kitchen had been stripped down to its linoleum floor. The deck restaining was coming along.

"At this rate, we'll be done in time for the open house next Saturday."

Thank You, Jesus.

After that, it was time for her to fade away. Nothing good could come out of letting Ming carry on with her.

Sure, he had kissed her this morning almost three times, but he was probably riding on some emotional high from whatever assignment he had been on all night.

No one could possibly kiss her and mean it, not with her scarred legs turning men off.

Clive had shown her that men wanted to see pretty things, and lovely legs were part of the pretty things. Someday, perhaps, someone would love her for who she was inside.

Maybe a blind man.

Then again, all a blind man had to do was put his hand on her legs, and he'd be grossed out. He'd feel the ugly scars and wrinkled skin that stretched all the way from her thighs down to her arches.

How could they possibly spend a single night together?

No. Marriage was out of the picture.

Maybe I'll get a pet.

Silently, she thanked God for her food as she leaned against a railing on the deck with her crew, eating fried chicken. They were chattering among themselves, but she was looking up at the sky and moving clouds. She didn't feel like talking this evening. She finished eating and went back inside the house.

Standing there in the living room was Ming, looking up at the new ceiling.

"I kinda miss my old ceiling," he said.

Sabine thought that Ming looked rested. In fact, he had bed hair. "How long have you been home?"

"Only the afternoon. I came home after lunch and took a nap."

"I'm sorry. My crew was here all day. It must've been noisy."

"No worries. I slept through it all. I can sleep through anything." Ming seemed proud of it.

"We're having fried chicken outside. Want some?" Sabine asked. "I brought plenty."

"Sure." Ming pointed at her. "Why are you wearing jeans?"

Sabine tried to think of something. "It's still chilly out."

"Really? Here I am, thinking it was something your sister said."

Sabine shrugged. "Sticks and stones."

"You don't believe that." Ming walked in front of her. "Words can heal, but they can also hurt."

Sabine's eyes stung. She blinked.

"Hey, want to see my stitches?" Ming lifted his shirt to reveal a large bandage. "I just need to—"

"No!" Sabine freaked out. "Put that down!"

"My wounds can beat up yours." He puffed up his chest.

Wounds. He said wounds.

He didn't say scars.

Sabine cleared her throat. "About this morning..."

"You owe me a third kiss."

"I owe you nothing. In fact, I think it's best if we—"

Ming's phone rang. "Hold that thought."

Sabine didn't want to hear, but Ming greeted Helen on the phone.

It seemed to Sabine that Ming and Helen worked well together. Helen deserved someone to love and to love her back as well. If there was anything between those two, Sabine decided she would not stand in the way.

It would be hard to watch. Helen had every-thing. A pretty face. A pretty body. No scars anywhere. Beautiful legs...

Whoa. Am I that shallow, God?

Forgive me.

She was about to walk away when she felt a tug on her hand. Ming held it. He shook his head as if he wanted her to stay.

He was still talking on the phone. "No, I can't work tonight. No way, Helen. I don't care. Ask Earl. He doesn't go to church in the morning. Pay him overtime. Whatever. I can't do it."

Sabine waited.

"No one says no to Helen," Sabine said after he hung up.

"Just did." Ming pocketed his phone and then held Sabine's hands in his. "About this morning, I meant it."

"I—uh..."

Ming placed a finger on Sabine's lips. "I have a few things to work through, and then I have something to tell you."

Sabine kissed his finger and lifted it away. "What? Tell me now."

"I'm not ready. You're not ready."

"Ready for what?"

Ming snapped his fingers. "Oh, that reminds me. Heidi and Diego want to see this house next week. When will you be free?"

Sabine frowned. "Don't change the subject. What was it you wanted to tell me?"

"I have to work out the words first."

Words? "Words to what?"

"Words to a song." Ming began whistling.

"Stop. What's going on? You're marrying my sister?"

Ming looked shocked. "Heaven forbid. It'll be like marrying a miniature Mama Hu."

"Did you just insult my entire family?" Sabine opened her mouth to say something else that popped into her head, but before she did that, she realized what Ming was doing. "Oh, I see. You're trying to distract me from finding out what you were trying to tell me. Tell me now, Aidan Ming Wei."

"Tell you soon." He lifted her chin.

When he pressed his lips oh so gently on hers, Sabine forgot the rest of her questions.

CHAPTER EIGHTEEN

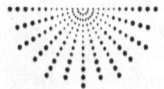

"*I*t's a small house," Heidi Wei-Flores said.

"With a big heart." Pastor Diego Flores followed his wife to the gutted kitchen.

Sabine couldn't read the meaning of it. Pastor Flores seemed to have noticed the questions on her face.

"Jesus is the heart of a home," Pastor Flores explained.

Yes. Jesus. Of course.

Sabine nodded. She decided she'd like to hear Pastor Flores preach next Sunday. Yesterday, she'd gone to the morning service at Riverside Chapel, but Pastor Flores had just returned from his Italian honeymoon and didn't preach.

Instead, the pastor's father had preached. The sermon had been difficult for her to process. It was about forgiveness. Well, Sabine knew Ephesians 4:32. She had memorized it in Sunday School when she had been a teenager.

And be kind to one another, tenderhearted, forgiving one another, even as God in Christ forgave you.

The elder Pastor Flores had challenged the congregation to apply it to friends, colleagues, and particularly family members.

She sighed.

Ming was right next to her. He mouthed, *What?*

Sabine smiled. "That is so true, Pastor Flores. Without Christ, the house is just a shell."

"Right." Pastor Flores stood at the wall in the living room. "If we were to buy this house, this wall has to go. I'm sorry you've already painted it."

Heidi went up to her husband. "Oh yes. Maybe we can bump out the wall and turn it into a large space here for parties, or maybe we could make a sunroom."

"If you put in folding doors, you could have an indoor-outdoor space most of the year," Sabine suggested.

"I love that idea," Heidi said. "What about in the winter? Will the doors be insulated enough?"

"Sure. The folding doors I use have a thermal system," Sabine explained.

"Sounds good to me, as long as we stay within budget." Pastor Flores wrapped an arm around Heidi.

There was something intimate about the exchange that wasn't lost on Sabine.

To love and to be loved. What a wonderful thing. Sigh.

A soft touch to her back between her shoulder blades reminded Sabine that such things were too wonderful for her.

She turned to see Ming again. He was sticking to her like glue, the smell of Irish Spring on his face and Bounce on his shirt. As per usual.

He was texting now. Curious, Sabine glanced over at his phone. She was tall enough to see the avatar on the large screen.

Helen again.

Sabine turned her attention back to her prospective buyers. "I emailed you the rough sketch of a possible expansion to the other end of the house. What do you think?"

"I like it," Pastor Flores said. "But we were thinking that, instead of a master suite, maybe we could have two bedrooms there. Then we could have guests."

"Yes, when Diego's brothers come visit," Heidi explained to Sabine. "If my in-laws don't have enough space for everyone, some of them could stay with us. Maybe at Christmas. If we have four bedrooms, then we could accommodate many people."

"Christmas will be here before you know it," Sabine said.

Ming looked up at her. "What about Christmas?"

Heidi punched him lightly on his arm on her way past him. "Oh my poor, lost big brother."

"Looks like everything's positive," Sabine said. "What about the drive to work?"

"We discussed that," Heidi said. "I'll have to drive about an hour round trip every day to get to campus, but I don't mind. I mean, I come home to the Atlantic Ocean."

"I work from home at the moment," Pastor Flores added. "Once we have a permanent building for Riverside Chapel, then we'll drive into Savannah together."

"Sounds like a plan." Sabine was glad the two of them had worked it out. Things could change once they had kids, but until then, this was the house they seemed to want.

"What do we do next?" Pastor Flores asked.

"Talk to your bank," Sabine said. "Decide how much you want to put down, and what a reasonable monthly payment would be. Meanwhile, I'll get you the contract to look at. You'll want a home inspection, even if this is Ming's house."

"I wish we could just pay in cash." Heidi looked at Pastor Flores. "I know we'd rather not be in debt. We just got married."

"We've prayed about it, and since we don't have any other debt, this is the only thing we'll have to work on," Pastor Flores said to her.

Sabine looked at wife, then husband, then wife. "If you want to do a fifteen-year loan and pay it off early, that could be an idea, especially before the kids come."

Ming didn't look up from his phone. "Kids? Did you say kids, Sabine?"

Sabine rolled her eyes.

"I have to run," Ming suddenly said as he dashed out of the living room.

Sabine felt a sense of loss when he left the house. She wasn't sure why she felt these deepening feelings. Sure, they had spent a lot of time together for almost two weeks, but then again, it wasn't enough time for her to feel attached to him, except for—

The kiss.

Well, Sabine had been kissed before.

Not by him.

But how many women had Ming kissed?

Surely a good-looking guy such as Ming had dated previously. What happened to all those women? They were not in his life now, were they?

Why should Sabine expect to be any different?

CHAPTER NINETEEN

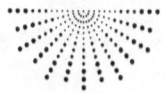

"*W*hat do you mean, Earl?" Ming rubbed the towel vigorously into his hair. His bedroom windows were open. He could hear the afternoon rain coming down. It was so loud it muffled the crashing waves on the shoreline.

He had come home around sunrise and had slept through noon. Lunch was a jam sandwich and a microwaved bowl of chicken soup from the can. He had just come out of the shower when one of Helen Hu's associates called.

"She's super nervous," Earl explained.

"You said that." Ming didn't like to hear people talking behind Sabine's back.

"She kept dropping her Glock when she was

loading the cartridge. It was pink, but it hit the table just like a regular piece."

Ming stopped everything he was doing.

Poor Sabine.

"She's still here if you want to come watch the show. Don't tell Helen we're taking bets on her sister. She'll kill us." Earl was laughing too much, too hard.

It irritated Ming to no end. "I can't believe you're kicking her while she's down."

"Why don't you come here and save your girl-friend, huh?"

Girlfriend?

One kiss does not a girlfriend make, or does it?

Ah, three kisses.

"We just started dating."

"Just started? The way you looked at her at Belford's could've fooled me. You two were *love-birding* at the table."

"We didn't do anything." Ming knew he didn't have to defend his dinner with Sabine. "We sat there in front of everybody and only talked. Besides, *lovebirding* is not a word."

"It is a verb now. It comes from the noun *love-bird*." Earl paused. "All right, man. Have to go. I might be losing my bet. Are you coming over here or not?"

"I don't know—"

"Hugo's whispering in her ear. He's the charmer. He's got your girl, Ming."

Hugo the Ego whispering what to Sabine?

"I'll be right over."

"I knew that would get your attention." Earl hung up.

It took a while for Ming to be *right over*. He had to replace the bandage on his side. Scabs were starting to form around the original entry and exit wounds below his ribs. But the extra stitches nearby made the whole area appear to be one big mess.

He was off pain medication. For that, he was grateful to God for answering his prayers and the prayers of his friends at Riverside Chapel.

Fifty minutes later, Ming was parked outside the River Run Indoor Range. His duffel bag of handguns, rifles, ammunition, safety goggles, earmuffs, and earplugs by his side, he ran through the rain into the shooting range.

He wasn't sure what to expect going in, but it seemed to be a normal Tuesday afternoon. Not the busiest time of the week, by any means, since it was during office hours.

Earl greeted him at the check-in desk while he was talking to Bryce La Salle's daughter. Bryce had bought the gun range from another businessman, and he had put his entire family to work there. His wife gave private instructions, his daughter helped at the cash register, and Bryce bought and sold firearms.

Sometimes Ming wondered if Bryce's brother, Camden, was going to work for him. Ming hadn't talked to Camden since September. After Camden had been fired from the FBI, he left town for good, it seemed.

Still, Ming had no doubt that someday Camden would return to Savannah. His roots were here, and so were his family and friends.

Earl pointed to the wall of ballistic windows nearby. Ming rubbernecked, and spotted tall and hunky Hugo on the other side of the window. He was standing too close to Sabine as they loaded more cartridges into their firearms.

Both were smiling.

The hair on Ming's arms rose.

He paid the fee for the hour and left his driver's license with Bryce's daughter, who was momentarily distracted by Earl's sweet talk. Ming had to ask her twice for a silhouette paper target before she heard him.

Ming imagined Hugo on the silhouette—

Forgive me, Lord!

"I changed my mind. Please give me the five bull's eyes instead." Ming cleared his throat. "Make that two."

He wasn't sure why he felt the need to challenge Hugo.

He put on his safety glasses and earmuffs over earplugs, and strutted through the two sets of soundproof doors to the row of firing bays, all empty except for the two occupied by Hugo and Sabine.

There was Hugo, oblivious to his presence. He had his big hands on Sabine's shoulders.

Ming lifted one side of his earmuffs to hear what Hugo had to say.

"Relax, Sabine. Get the tension out."

It was all Ming could take.

Earl held his arm back.

Ming didn't realize Earl had followed him.

Earl put his hand on Ming's arm, and shook his head.

Ming decided to stay put against the wall, if for no other reason than to wait for his turn to humiliate Hugo. And to cool down. Mumbling under his breath, he recited James 1:20.

For the wrath of man does not produce the righteousness of God.

Right before his eyes, Sabine shrugged off Hugo before he could massage her shoulders.

Hugo's mouth opened and closed. Ming wanted

to know what he was saying. He lifted his earmuffs again since nobody was shooting at the moment.

"I can help you be more accurate." Hugo spoke loudly as he pointed to the silhouette on the paper target some ten yards away. "See that chest area on the paper thingy? That's where you need to hit."

Sabine smiled.

Ming couldn't believe it. *Don't encourage him, Sabine!*

Sabine stepped back, giving Hugo room at the bay. He spread out his legs like a gunfighter, and steadily aimed at the silhouette.

Ming covered his ears with his earmuffs and waited.

Hugo was good. But it was only fifteen yards.

It was Sabine's turn now, with her pink Glock. Ming waited to see how long it would take for her to see him leaning against the back wall, plotting Hugo's demise.

She stopped as she walked toward her bay. She turned around, and her eyes lit up. "Ming!"

Ming couldn't hear her, but he could read lips some. He waved, telling himself to calm down.

Sabine walked toward him, lifting her pink—pink!—earmuffs. She reached over to his earmuffs and spoke into his ear. "Did you bring your Glock or Sig?"

How did she—

Oh yeah.

Ming had mentioned it the day she had delivered him the set of photographs from Helen. Ming was surprised that Sabine had remembered. He wondered what else she remembered him saying.

Better be careful what I say.

"Yeah, I brought them. Why?" Ming asked.

"What kind of Glock do you have?"

"A 23."

"May I borrow it?"

Say what?

"Well..." Ming didn't know how to respond.

"My mag can only hold six rounds." Sabine's palm was out. "Please?"

"Uh...okay." Ming found an empty spot on a table nearby. He opened his gun case, and realized that he hadn't had time this morning to load his clips. Helen had used up her magazines and then his while he sat in the surveillance van all night. To be fair, he had been sleeping all morning.

Sabine was standing so closely to Ming that he picked up a floral scent of some sort mixed in with the smell of gunpowder. He did everything he could to focus on his speed loader as he put the rest of the rounds into the ten-round clip.

Still, he refused to hand over his loaded Glock to Sabine. "Why don't I have a go?"

"This is between Hugo and me, Ming."

"You're not going to drop it, are you?" Ming asked.

Nearby, Earl let out a hearty laugh.

Sabine's eyes widened. She gave Earl a look that reminded Ming of how Mama Hu glared at people. Earl backed away, palms up.

Sabine pointed to the paper target on the floor. "May I use that too?"

"Five bull's eye targets." Hugo came over, laughing like a goat.

"What do you think, Hugo?" Sabine picked up the sheets. "Two sheets here. Nice. How about we try to get five bull's eyes at fifteen yards?"

Ming wondered what Sabine was up to.

"Why don't we try ten yards?" Hugo waved his hand about. "That red dot thingy might be too hard for you."

"How long have you worked at Hu Knows, Hugo?" Sabine asked.

"Going on a year."

"You've never met my dad then."

"No."

"He used to call it the red dot thingy too."

"He did?"

Sabine nodded. "Let's get going. I have a house showing I have to get to."

"Winner gets a kiss?" Hugo looked serious when he said it.

Ming's blood began to boil. *What kiss?*

"No. No prizes for winning except having won," Sabine explained as they walked toward their bays to set up their targets.

Ming prayed silently for Sabine. He prayed that she wouldn't shoot herself or him or Hugo—well, as for Hugo...

Forgive me again, Lord.

He watched Sabine and Hugo adjust their earmuffs and replace their silhouettes with the bull's eyes paper targets on hanging holders. The targets moved away from the bay counter.

Fifteen yards.

"Ready?" Ming shouted as loudly as he could. "Go!"

Ming cringed at the idea of Sabine giving Hugo a winner's kiss, before he realized she had finished pumping ten rounds one after another into the five circles.

Ming leaned back against the wall for support.

I have no words.

Sabine pushed the button on the wall to retrieve her paper target.

Delighted, she came straight to him, the paper flying in the air.

Ming's eyes couldn't get any wider. She had only missed three.

Three.

Is it possible?

Hugo strutted toward them, his paper target in front of him for all to see.

"Dude, you missed four," Ming announced, stepping between Sabine and Hugo, just in case someone decided to carry out the promise of a winner's kiss.

"Yeah. So how many did you miss, Sabine?" Hugo asked, leaning.

"She missed three." Ming lifted the paper for him to see.

Hugo squinted. His eyes went back and forth between the two sheets. He pointed to his. "I nicked that one bull's eye. It's a tie. I think an eyelash was in my eye."

"Yeah. That's got to be it," Ming said.

"I demand a rematch." Hugo was serious.

"I'll have Mom cook you dinner." Sabine laughed.

Ming held back a grin. There was no way Mama Hu was going to cook again. The last time she did it, the entire fire station showed up to put out the smoke in her historic house.

Sabine returned Ming's Glock to him, and started packing up her gun case. "I have to run. Have to drive to Tybee."

Ming followed Sabine out of the bay area, while

a dejected Hugo remained behind for more target practice.

Sabine put away her earmuffs and safety glasses. Ming thought she looked pretty with her hair tied up in a chignon. She usually had it in a ponytail.

"I gather Hugo will never bother you again," Ming said.

"He's a nice guy. Don't worry."

"Nice guy? Now I'm really worried."

As they walked toward the counter to retrieve their driver's licenses, a realization hit Ming. "Your dad taught you to shoot."

"Since I was twelve. He thought I would take over Hu Private Investigations, now known to you as Hu Knows."

Ming had another thought. "The pink Glock isn't your first handgun."

Sabine smiled. "I never said it was. I just said it was new."

"Right."

What else don't I know about you, Sabine Hu?

CHAPTER TWENTY

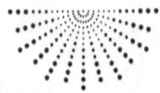

*S*abine was pleased to find out that Ming's sister and husband were in a very good financial place. They had no credit card debt, no car payment, and no student loans. Apparently Heidi had used her inheritance money her deceased parents had left her to pay for school.

Between Pastor Flores and Heidi, they had enough savings to put down at least twenty percent, with money left over for a home inspection and an appraisal. They both had jobs, with Heidi's research and teaching job at the University of Coastal Georgia earning her several times more income than Pastor Flores.

They were ready to buy.

Even though their bank would take a few more days to approve their loan for the fifteen-year mortgage, it was almost a sure thing. For that reason, the Floreses wanted to talk to Sabine's general contractor about bumping out Ming's house on both sides. One side would be for the indoor-outdoor sunroom, and the other would be for two new bedrooms.

No rooftop deck, unfortunately.

No matter. A sale is a sale.

When Sabine arrived at the house Monday, it had been a week since she had last seen Ming. He had been busy with Helen in some sort of project tracking down an international fugitive holed up in coastal Georgia. Sabine didn't ask. Didn't want to know. Didn't care.

She knew Ming wasn't going to make the meeting. He had pretty much left it up to his sister to talk to Sabine about the home renovations, the colors, and the decor. Fortunately, they didn't have to change the cream color of the walls. Repainting would cost more than necessary.

Everything else remained the same. It was interesting to Sabine that Heidi and Ming had similar tastes. Sabine couldn't say the same about her and Helen. They were like night and day.

Sabine heard laughter echoing from the backyard.

Through the living room and kitchen, she made her way to the gathering on the porch. Three people were chatting and laughing in Spanish and English. A smiling Heidi, Pastor Flores, and Sabine's old friend and go-to general contractor, Tobias Vega, were cutting it up.

"Toby!" She hugged her old friend, who had driven up today from St. Simon's Island to discuss how to renovate the Floreses' new home.

Really, he didn't have to come up here; his Vega Constructions' branch office in Savannah could have handled it. But Tobias said he hadn't seen Sabine in a while, and they agreed to have dinner afterward to catch up.

"Happy birthday." Tobias Vega handed Sabine a card.

"It's not my birthday," Sabine said.

"Sorry I'm late by six months."

Sabine laughed. She opened the envelope. Sandwiched into the birthday card was a gift card from Belford's.

Belford's. Where she and Ming had dinner the other night.

"Thank you." Sabine stuffed the envelope into her purse. "I see you've met Pastor and Mrs. Flores."

Tobias nodded. "Got here early."

"How's traffic on 95?"

"Pretty good. You owe me dinner. Don't forget." Tobias pointed at Sabine. "But you can't use your gift card."

"Glad you could come up here on such a short notice."

Pastor Flores interrupted them. "Maybe we owe Toby dinner instead."

"I'll take you up on that another time," Tobias said. "It'll be at least two months before we can finish the extensions."

Sabine didn't know that Ming was standing behind her until Heidi waved.

Awkwardly, Sabine introduced Ming to Tobias. The men eyed each other.

What's wrong with them?

"Okay, I'm sure we all have to be places, so why don't you two show Toby what you want done, and go from there?" Sabine asked.

Pastor Flores and Heidi ushered Tobias down the steps to the side of the house where the storage shed was. More Spanish and English words echoed in the ocean air. Above them, the sun was still up in the sky.

Ming leaned down and pecked Sabine on her cheek. "Hey, haven't seen you all week."

"How is it going?"

"Poorly."

"I'm sorry. How can I pray?" Sabine's hand reflexively went toward Ming's, but she pulled it back.

"Nothing wrong with holding hands," Ming

said.

When Sabine didn't reply, Ming added, "Don't want to be seen with me in public?"

"It's not that."

"Or just in front of Tobias there."

Sabine followed Ming's gaze. The three of them were still talking outside the storage shed. Tobias flashed his laser distance measurer.

"Toby? We've known each other for years," Sabine explained.

"Toby, is it?"

"You're jealous."

"Nah."

Sabine ran her hand up and down Ming's arm. "Liar."

"I'm not. I don't know what it is, but I don't want any other guy with you."

"If I go to a business meeting with Toby, will you be upset?"

"No."

"A business dinner meeting?"

Sabine watched Ming's face. His eyes flickered just a tad. She smiled.

"I've spent nights sitting in a van with Helen. How do you feel about that?"

Sabine glanced behind Ming. Beyond the deck, the trio had disappeared. They were probably assessing how to add two bedrooms to the side of the house.

Sabine pulled Ming's shirt. He came forward. She didn't have to lift her toes much. She was wearing platform flip-flops, and they were almost at eye level. She ran her fingers along the base of his neck.

"I would never do this with another guy." With the other hand, she gently pulled his head toward hers.

She tasted his lips. "Mmm... Coffee. Hazelnut?"

Ming was too busy returning her kiss.

Sabine came up for air. "Are you getting enough rest?"

"Why do you ask?"

"You've been working nights."

"I don't have a choice. I wish I had a day job."

"I'll pray for you."

"Please." Ming tightened his arms around her waist.

Gently, Sabine melded into his embrace. "What are we, Ming?"

"An item."

"Are we?"

"I thought so. I think so. Are you having second thoughts?"

"I don't think I've even had first thoughts. Not to completion, anyway."

"No worries, Sabine. We're just getting to know each other. Funny. The more I work with your sister, the more I think I know you."

Sabine was alarmed. This couldn't be good. She stepped back. "What made you say that?"

"Helen has been telling me about the day you were born and how she hated having a baby sister who got all the attention."

"She's overreacting."

"She didn't want a younger sister, a sister who then became model-tall and beautiful. I have to concur with her, Sabine. You are beautiful."

"No—"

Ming's finger was on her lips again. "Shhh. I'm not done. Helen said she hated herself for being short and stubby."

"Stubby? Helen is not stubby, by any stretch of the imagination. She's petite."

"She hates her five-inch stilettos. She fears getting ankle sprains every time she wears them."

"Then she shouldn't."

"What I told her! Who cares if she's only five feet tall?"

Poor Helen. Sabine had no idea her sister had such a low self-esteem.

Oh, who am I to talk?

"She hasn't forgiven herself for the wreck that ruined your career and almost took your life,"

Ming said. "She's mad at God for not stopping her."

Sabine was stunned.

I blame her, and she blames God? "It's not God's fault."

"She thinks you will never forgive her. Every time she sees you, she dies a little."

"She said that?"

Ming nodded.

Sabine's palm flew to her mouth.

I have to forgive my sister.

Ming gently squeezed Sabine's arm. "You and Helen need to talk. You two have a lot to work out."

Sabine nodded.

"Diego said that unforgiveness is like flesh-eating bacteria. It will eat you alive."

Eeek!

"You can't have God's love and hatred at the same time."

"I don't hate my sister." It was the truth. Sabine loved her family. She couldn't stand Helen some-times, but they were still family. She couldn't imagine *hating* Helen, but she did try to avoid her. Not the same thing, right?

"You haven't forgiven her."

"We don't talk about it."

"It's hanging over your head."

"Yes."

"And hers too."

"Oh." Sabine knew then how she was going to spend the gift card that Tobias had given her.

~

"Stay away from Sabine." Mama Hu was adamant.

I don't need this now.

She had caught Ming at a very bad time. The doctor had insisted that he rested at home, but tonight was the last night of their surveillance, and the last time Ming would be paid for a while.

The pain in his side was returning. He hadn't had much sleep the night before, and not much more sleep would come tonight.

We have to catch the fugitive before he goes after anyone else.

And now this.

"Why?" Ming snapped back. He had tried not to be rude to Mama Hu. Ever. But now he had broken his own rule.

It was eleven o'clock at night. He had spent the last three hours wondering what Sabine was doing driving off with Tobias Vega, her general contractor. Granted, they had taken two vehicles, but he had overheard that they were having a business dinner together. Tonight.

What did a *business dinner* mean for Sabine and a guy?

It irritated Ming to no end.

The last thing he needed was Mama Hu giving him this sort of send-off.

"She's fragile, Ming." Mama Hu's voice was laced with concern.

Fragile?

She didn't look fragile at River Run Indoor Range the other day.

"I don't want to see her hurt again."

"Again? How?" It bothered Ming that someone had hurt Sabine before. *Well, let me bash his face in.*

"She's been through a lot. Her last boyfriend was a jerk. Left her while she was lying there in the hospital."

"I won't." Ming kept walking. Mama Hu still stuck to him like chewing gum.

Helen was talking to someone outside the van in the garage. She waved to him. He nodded.

"That's what all you men say."

"Not all of us." Ming stopped at the door. "Look, Mama Hu. Please understand. I care for your daughter very much. She's a tough cookie, but we're looking out for each other."

"Are you?"

"Yep. We're buddies."

Kissing buddies. Whatever that means.

CHAPTER TWENTY-ONE

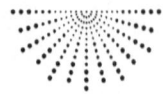

*A*ppraisal done, home loan approved, inspection completed, closing over, Ming's house now belonged to his sister and brother-in-law.

While he grieved the loss of his small footprint in the world—this little rectangular piece of the beach by the Atlantic Ocean—he knew that his house would be in good hands.

Heidi and Diego would turn it into a retreat and a place of ministry, neither of which Ming had time to do, nor the calling to fulfill at this career-building time of his life.

By six in the evening, his friends—and those of Heidi's and Diego's—had filed into his backyard. Diego and a couple of guys from church were setting up folding tables to line up from end to end, forming one long table parallel to the back of the tiny house.

Abilene and Nadine from church arranged plastic chairs on both sides of the outdoor table. There was Heidi, placing small vases of floral arrangements on the tables.

Ming thanked God it wasn't raining and that the temperature was in the sixties, because it was going to be hot out here standing at the grill.

A can of soda appeared in front of him as he was fanning the coals. He recognized the maroon fingernails. He mustered up a smile and peered up through his Ray-Bans, his own eyes shaded.

"Need any help?" Sabine asked.

"No, but I don't mind the company." Ming poured hot coals from the charcoal chimney onto the Weber grill grate. He fanned the flame.

They looked back at the house.

"That's a cozy little cottage," Sabine said.

Ming opened his can of soda. "Yep. So sorry to see it go, but I know my sister will take care of it and make better use of it than I ever could as a single guy."

"Still, it's possible to be attached to a place."

Or a person. "I guess."

"What are you going to do about your housing situation?"

"I don't know," Ming said truthfully. "I'll rent something."

"How's the sale of your company to Helen?"

"She's not discussing it until this case is solved." Ming wasn't sure how much to tell Sabine, but he felt that he could trust her. Besides, the two sisters didn't speak.

"I guess this is it." Sabine smiled sadly.

"What do you mean?" Ming thought he could hear an alarm ringing in his ears. Was Sabine backing away from their budding relationship?

"I sold your house. It's up to Pastor Flores and Heidi now to work with Toby's company to renovate it. My job ended at the closing. I'm done."

"As for you and me..." Ming's voice drifted off as his fingers outlined her chin. "We're not done."

They stood there studying each other against the sounds of the surf and seabirds around them.

Before he could do anything, Diego and Roger approached them with two trays of giant hamburgers.

"Roger, my friend! You're back from Mumbai!" Ming bear-hugged Roger Patel as Diego walked around them to the grill. "When did you get back?"

"This afternoon. I'm still jet-lagged, so if I fall asleep at the dinner table, pardon me—oh, who is this lovely lady?" Roger walked up to Sabine. "I'm Dr. Roger Patel. What's your beautiful name?"

Ming rolled his eyes behind Roger, and it made Sabine laugh.

"Sabine Hu, a friend of Ming's." She shook his hand.

A friend of Ming's?

Ming didn't like that at all. He wanted their relationship to go further, beyond friendship, to something more. Standing there watching Sabine chatter away with Roger with such ease made him somewhat—

Jealous?

Roger always made the ladies comfortable with his impeccable bedside manner.

"So are you a medical doctor or is your title academic?" Sabine asked as Roger's hand cupped her elbow.

Ming didn't like that at all. *Get your own girl, Roger!*

"MD, ma'am, but these days I'm not actually practicing much anymore." Roger showed his straight teeth. "I'm the director of the Savannah Senior Living Resort."

Ming was momentarily distracted when he saw Diego battling the Weber. The pastor was clumsy with the tongs. "Here, let me take care of that."

Ming rearranged the hamburgers on the grate. While it was a change of pace to have burgers tonight, Ming had wanted to impress Sabine with his grilled salmon burgers.

"May I introduce you to all of Ming's friends?" Roger asked Sabine.

Ming didn't say a word. He tried to read Sabine's reaction but failed.

"I'll save you a seat, okay?" Sabine said to him as he walked away with Roger.

Ming nodded. He decided not to open his mouth. He feared saying things to Roger—or worse, to Sabine—that he would regret later. Watching them walk around the long outdoor dining tables bothered Ming somehow.

It continued to bother him after they had disappeared into the back door of his—not anymore!—house. Ming had a good mind to let someone else take care of the grilling, but this was his Weber. Nobody touched his Weber.

Weber or Sabine?

Yikes.

Ming decided he couldn't afford to be the laughingstock among his friends if he burned the hamburger. "Lord, please go in there and keep Roger's hands off Sabine."

Would God answer that kind of prayer?

It seemed frivolous.

If Sabine was meant to be for Ming, they'd be together, right?

Ming determined not to worry. He was so lost in thought that he didn't realize Diego was still standing there. Arms folded, his friend, confidant, pastor, and now brother-in-law, seemed amused.

"That bad, huh?" Diego said.

"What do you mean?" Ming played coy.

"Some prayer there."

Ming said nothing.

"You said it aloud. Been there myself, but at least I pray in my car where nobody but God hears me," Diego said. "You couldn't stand to see Sabine walk off with Roger."

"You mean Mr. Handsome?"

"Ladies' man, that Dr. Roger."

"Multitalented physician, businessman, and stand-in preacher?"

"And our friend," Diego added.

"Not if he takes Sabine away from me." Ming tried to keep his voice low.

He regretted saying that almost immediately. Beyond the sea oat dunes, the waves crashed, as if to concur with his selfish statement.

"She's not yours. She belongs to God. If God wants you two to be together, no one can stop Him. Ask me how I know."

"We just started out. It's hard to tell which way we're going, you know."

"All the more reason not to hold on to her too tightly."

Ming nodded. He checked the temperature of the burgers and decided to let them cook a bit more before he flipped them. He closed the grill lid.

"Sometimes we try to impress people," Diego began.

"I smell a sermon coming." Ming chuckled. "But go on. I want to hear."

"Sometimes we try to impress people, but do we make an effort to impress God? 'Delight yourself also in the Lord, and He shall give you the desires of your heart.' Psalm 37:4."

Ming opened the grill cover. "I know that verse."

"Often we know a lot of verses, but we don't apply them. Ask me how I know." Diego laughed.

"You too?"

"Yeah, with Heidi. Remember?" Diego's gaze was distant. "I pushed her away, when God wanted me to welcome her."

Ming wanted to say something, but his iPhone pinged. Then it pinged again. And again.

He groaned. He had to take the call.

Sure enough. It was Helen. She wanted him to call her pronto.

Frankly, he was tired of Helen texting him twenty-four seven. He wanted the job over and done with, even if there was no future beyond the paycheck he would receive for his work the night before.

"Want me to get you a clean platter?" Diego asked.

"Yeah. That would be good. Thanks."

Diego turned back. "Hey, I almost forgot. Got a call from Cam. He's in Dayton, Ohio. He asked about you."

"He did?" Ming was glad to hear it. He hadn't had any time to keep up with Camden La Salle. "I need to call him. See how he's doing."

"He's still grieving Daljeet. But he got over being mad at himself."

"What's he doing now?" Ming asked.

"Stocking shelves at Walmart."

"Glad he's working." Ming wondered if Camden would come back to Savannah and—

Nah.

Ming had already decided to sell Savannah River Investigations, and that was all there was to it. He was done running his own business. It was time to work for someone else. Let them worry about income, payroll taxes, red tape, whatever.

He wished he wasn't selling his company at all. He had tried again to talk to Helen about it, but Helen was noncommittal. In a way, it would be best if he didn't sell it to Helen's company and go to work for her. The more he worked with Helen, the more complicated his relationship with Sabine would be. He felt that Sabine couldn't be open and frank with him on her own terms when Helen went behind her sister's back and talked about her.

Speaking of Helen, he still had to call her.

What does she want?

Sighing loudly, Ming swiped his iPhone to take care of business.

CHAPTER TWENTY-TWO

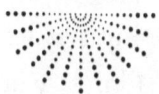

*S*abine loved this outdoor dining setup. It looked simple with the vinyl tablecloth and plastic chairs, but there was a rustic elegance to it. She could try something like this on her rooftop patio, but it wouldn't be the same.

Here on the grass, next to the dunes by the sea, the atmosphere changed with the sound of ocean waves and the Atlantic breeze coming onshore.

Sabine felt as though she were at a retreat.

If only Ming would stop pouting.

Sitting next to her, Ming hadn't said a word through the appetizers and hamburger meal. Now they were eating Pastor Flores's apparently famous cupcakes, and still, Ming hadn't said anything more than incomplete sentences, grunts, and groans.

"Are your stitches bothering you?" Sabine asked.

Across the table, Heidi spoke up. "He should've had those removed a couple of weeks ago, right?"

"No worries, sis," Ming said.

Sabine realized then that Ming hadn't told his sister about the new injuries he had incurred while Heidi and Pastor Flores were on their Italian honeymoon.

Heidi glared at Ming. "We'll talk later."

"Uh-huh." Ming quickly stuffed more cupcakes into his mouth.

Well, if Ming didn't want to talk to her, then she'd talk to someone else. Sabine turned her attention to the person on her right.

"So, you're an artist. Watercolor only?" Sabine asked Abilene Dupree, whom she had met the first Sunday she visited Riverside Chapel.

Abilene put a finger up as she continued chewing.

Sabine had eaten one cupcake, but zucchini wasn't her thing. There were other cupcakes being passed around at the other end of the long table, but she'd have to wait for the tray to get to her. The cupcakes weren't labeled, and she didn't want to make a scene about not liking zucchini after everyone had been raving about Pastor Flores's amazing baking skills.

Abilene drank some water. "I do it all. Water-color, oil, pastels, mixed media, whatever I feel like doing."

"Someone said earlier that you have some paintings for sale at Simon's Gallery."

Abilene nodded. "I'm getting ready to start another series for Simon soon. He wants me to paint local scenes around Savannah and Tybee."

"I would love to hang some paintings in my house. It's kind of stark at the moment. Maybe a splash of color here and there might be nice."

"Simon has a lot of colorful paintings," Abilene said.

Ming chose that moment to take his plate and leave the table. Sabine glanced over to see him head toward some people carrying a football toward the beach. It was dusk, with some daylight left. After dark, there was no light on the beach, and she doubted they could play football out there long.

Ming chatted with them as they laughed and walked across the boardwalk.

So he can speak.

Just not to me this evening.

What's going on, Ming?

Sabine let it roll off her. Her legs felt tired. She was ready to go home and rest her weary bones. Maybe read a book or swim in her heated pool.

"Do you do commission work as well?" Sabine asked Abilene.

"Yes." She named her price.

Still life didn't sound too expensive to Sabine. "If I get permission from Pastor Flores and Heidi, and they say yes, could you draw this house and the beach before they bump out both sides of the wall and change the way the house looks?"

"It faces the beach, so I might have to get it at an angle if you want to see both the house and the beach," Abilene said.

"I suppose you can't draw it from the front yard either because you can't see the beach from there, with all the hedges and the fence." Sabine waved her arms about.

"I'll see what I can do. When do you want this painting?"

"How soon can you do it? I'm thinking I prefer oil. Let's talk some more." Sabine exchanged emails with Abilene.

"It won't take long as soon as I begin," Abilene said. "I'm not sure if I can begin until April, but I'll come out here in the next few days to take some pictures."

"If Heidi and Pastor Flores agree. I'll ask them and let you know. We'll talk about payments then." Sabine felt a nerve pull in her left leg. She had been on her feet too long. "Well, I'm heading home. Had a long day. Nice to see you again, Abilene."

"Same here. See you around."

Sabine left Abilene sitting there eating her third or fourth cupcake. As she stood up, she turned to face the ocean. She could see the bobbing heads of some of the people playing football on the beach on the other side of the dune. But she could not spot Ming.

Oh well.

As Sabine walked to her SUV parked on the curb, she called Mom. No answer. Perhaps she had found another chaperone to accompany her out for the evening. Or she had the phone muted or turned off.

No matter.

Sabine was too tired to chat with anyone. She only called because she was obligated to make sure Mom was okay. She sent Mom a text to ask how her day went. Then she pocketed her phone and fished for her SUV keys.

Less than forty minutes later, Sabine was taking the elevator up to her penthouse condominium.

Five minutes after changing into her swimsuit, she stepped into her rooftop pool. She swam a few laps until the tension in her body eased and her bones felt massaged. The dull pain in her left thigh dissipated, and the throbbing in her right ankle eased.

Both were reminders of the trauma she had endured in the fiery wreck that had killed one of her sister's employees and nearly left Sabine disabled.

Three years of therapy.

And a lifetime of endurance.

Sabine swam one more lap. The butterfly stroke wasn't her favorite swimming style, but it made her use her upper body and arm muscles more.

She reached the edge of the pool, thinking she'd go to bed early tonight. She held onto the mosaic sides of the pool, wiped water droplets off her face, and found herself staring into the nozzle of a silencer.

CHAPTER TWENTY-THREE

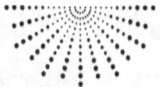

"The only way into my sister's condo is through the roof." Helen Hu was practically screaming into her phone. "You're telling me that nobody—not a single soul—saw or heard anything—a chopper, maybe—land on her patio? What about grease spots? Jet fuel residues? Something?"

Ming sat on a nearby table, arms folded as he listened to the tirade.

When Helen poured coffee into a mug, then lifted the carafe to her mouth, Ming tried to warn her, but she snarled at him and made him back off.

It only took seconds for Helen to slosh hot coffee onto her wool jacket. She screamed into the phone. "Look what you made me do, Gorman!"

She put down the carafe and picked up the coffee mug.

Ming thought her face had reddened.

"We're talking about my sister and mother, the most important people in the world to me. Do you understand?" Helen didn't wait too long for an answer, it seemed to Ming. "Fan out, Gorman. Hire more off-duty officers if you want to. You have my permission. I want the entire southeast picked apart. Ten hours. How far can you drive in ten hours? That's the radius we're focusing on!"

She hung up. Paced the floor in her five-inch platform espadrilles.

"Maybe you should sit down," Ming suggested. "The FBI, GBI, and SCMPD are all working on it."

"Yeah, keep telling yourself that."

"I am. It's how I cope, Helen." If the Federal Bureau of Investigations and the Georgia Bureau of Investigations were on the case, then the Savannah-Chatham Metropolitan Police Department had way more help than Hu Knows and Savannah River Investigations could provide.

But would their efforts be enough?

Helen stopped in front of Ming. Even with her platform shoes, she was still at least nine or ten inches shorter than Ming.

On the other hand, Sabine was much taller. The

way he could look into her eyes and see her lips without dipping his head down much—

"You like my sister, don't you?" Helen said in that clinical voice of hers.

More than *like*. "She and I have something going, I thought."

"Then you'll want to have this." Helen pulled out something from her jacket pocket. She placed it in Ming's open palm.

It was Sabine's cross.

"Dad gave it to Sabine before he passed away."

"I know." Ming held it up.

"They found it in her walk-in closet next to her wet swimsuit. She usually doesn't wear jewelry when she swims."

Ming was glad to hear Helen talk about Sabine in the present tense. "She's in God's hands."

Helen laughed. Then stopped herself. "Don't get me wrong. I'm not mocking God. My sister, she's religious in many ways, and now her faith will be put to the test."

For sure. Still, Ming didn't want Sabine to suffer. She had gone through enough.

I'm always collateral damage.

Sabine's words at the party, that party in which they had almost danced behind the potted plants and tall pillars. The memories of their evening together brought a sad smile to Ming's face.

Collateral damage.

Something about that tried to poke through Ming's thoughts, but he couldn't put a finger on it.

"You have my blessing," Helen said.

"Thanks." Then again, Ming knew he didn't need Helen's blessing.

I need God's blessing instead.

Helen wiped sweat off her forehead. She went to the windows. Opened them wide.

The sounds of downtown Savannah poured into the room. Vehicle engines from the morning rush hour, a few honks here and there. Some sort of kettledrum music from across the street. A distant airplane up in the sky.

It was another Wednesday morning in the coastal town.

Yet it wasn't another morning.

Ming had been up half the night with his FBI and Interpol liaisons. So far, nothing.

He wished—

So many things juxtaposed in his mind. *Why didn't I tell her last night?*

He had wanted to while they were sitting together at the outdoor dinner in his backyard.

He had wanted so badly to say something to her about where he wanted their relationship to go, but he couldn't muster the courage.

It had frustrated him that he didn't have the words to tell her how he felt about her.

In the end, he had decided not to talk to her.

That had been a dumb move.

Sabine had moved on by then, chatting with Abilene about art and stuff. Ming had decided to leave the table to gather his thoughts. Then he had been pulled into flag football on the beach. By the time the sun had set, Sabine was gone.

When Abilene had told him Sabine had felt tired, Ming had decided not to text or call her.

I was trying to give her some space.

One more regret.

I should have just told her.

CHAPTER TWENTY-FOUR

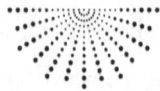

*S*abine opened her eyes to dim lights and the pungent smell of a dog needing a bath got closer to her. She heard a moan but was unable to move her head. There was a kink in her neck. Pain shot up and down her legs.

Where...

Crisscrossing metal bars rose into the air and disappeared. She felt dizzy, and closed her eyes.

The moan became louder.

Sabine winced as she turned her head slightly. Somewhere among the metal bars she spotted black hair, maybe five or six feet away. "Mom?"

"Sabine!" The voice was raspy but unmistakable.

"Mom! Where are we?" Sabine tried to sit up. "Oh...I can't move my legs."

"Take it easy, Sabine. Rest. Wait for the tranq to wear off."

Mom should know about tranquilizers. She had used them a couple of times on unsuspecting suspects. She used to run Hu Knows, Inc., but now she had handed the day-to-day activities to Helen.

Mom still gave Sabine flak about bailing out of the family business.

Sabine reached for her thighs, and massaged them. She mustered what feeble strength she had to adjust her position. That was when she realized she was wearing pajamas.

She touched the ground around her. It was dusty and grimy. Some sort of flooring?

When her eyes adjusted to the dim light, she realized that she was sitting on dirty linoleum floor, surrounded by tall metal bars that reached up to the low ceiling with one small lamp hanging from it.

I'm in a cage somewhere.

"Sabine, you okay now?" Mom asked softly.

Sabine looked in Mom's direction. Beyond her cage, there was a narrow walkway. Then there was another cage with Mom in it.

"What happened?" Sabine asked feebly.

"They want me. They've come for me, after all these years."

"Mom."

"I'm sure of it. They won't let me rest. My sins

have caught up with me. I wish I'd never..." Mom's voice trailed off.

"Mom, are you sure it's you they want?" Sabine asked.

"It's certainly not *you*."

Ironically, it didn't make Sabine feel better. She closed her eyes.

She remembered swimming in her pool. Several masked men—or women—brandishing various firearms made her get out of the pool, dry off, and change into her pajamas.

Then something sharp pinched her neck—syringe?—and she couldn't remember anything more.

And now she had a throbbing headache.

Lord Jesus, help us.

She prayed away her headache, but it was still there. She also prayed for Ming, that he wouldn't worry.

Worry?

Sabine wondered if Ming was worried at all. It was terrible that the last thing she remembered of him was his pouting. If he was jealous of her interaction with Roger and other men from Riverside Chapel, wouldn't that be his problem and not hers? In her line of work as a real estate agent, she had to talk to men.

Maybe that wasn't it.

Something else was bothering Ming. "I guess I'll never find out."

"Find out what?" Mom's voice pierced the air.

"Nothing. Why are we really here, Mom?" Why had she been abducted from her house? How did they get in? She had locked the doors and set the alarm, hadn't she?

Sabine tried to trace her steps all the way back to her basement parking garage, but drew a blank. Nobody had followed her. The entire building seemed quiet.

Oh. They were already inside my house.

That had to be the only explanation.

"How did they get into my house, Mom?" Sabine asked.

"Rooftop, is my guess. They could land a chopper on your terrace." Mom had that faraway look, as if remembering the good old days when Dad had been alive.

"So you think they waited inside until I got home."

"They could also pick your door lock. It would be easy. Told you to get a better door."

"I have an alarm system, Mom."

"Even your sister can bypass it." Mom managed what sounded like a guffaw. "I think, after this, you should consider selling that penthouse."

"Why? I like it."

"Bad luck."

"I'm a Christian, Mom. I don't believe in luck. I believe that God is sovereign. God is in control. God is going to work out all these for our good."

"You said God three times. Three times is good luck, as you know."

"Mom, you can't mix superstitions with Christianity. Either you believe God is God, or chances rule your life."

"I'll take my chances."

Sabine rolled her eyes. "Don't get us both killed, Mom."

Sabine felt dizzy again.

She closed her eyes, and smelled a dirty dog.

CHAPTER TWENTY-FIVE

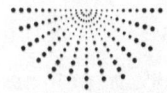

"Thank you for coming to this emergency prayer meeting," Diego Flores said to his friends.

Sitting next to Diego on her camp chair, Heidi was softly crying.

Ming put an arm around his sister's shoulders. He didn't know why she was crying. She hardly knew Sabine. Perhaps the impending danger had triggered memories of their parents' endangerment and deaths, and it affected her now.

He hushed her as Diego went on. "We're going to read a few verses, and then we're going to split up and pray in groups of twos and threes. I thought we'd go around a circle to pray sequentially, but I see that half our church members have shown up, and so in the interest of time, we'll pray concurrently."

Ming was touched that so many people had shown up to pray for the safety of Sabine and her mother.

It had only been two nights ago that everyone had seen Sabine alive. She had gotten to know more people at Riverside Chapel, and they had remembered her visiting the Sunday church services.

They had welcomed her with open arms. Invited her to lunch.

She was part of their family now.

"After we pray, we're going to eat. Thank you to everyone who brought hot food," Diego said.

"What's a prayer meeting without food?" Roger said, nudging Ming's other arm.

Ming wanted to punch his old friend, but he knew Roger meant well. He was trying to lighten things up a bit. Roger had his own ways about things, though Ming didn't always understand his friend.

Still, Roger was Roger. He had cancelled his evening events and had shown up for Ming.

Or is it for Sabine?

Well, if they didn't seek God, neither of them would have Sabine.

"I'll pray with you," Roger said to Ming. "That okay?"

"Ah...sure." *Let's see what he says to God.*

"Let's go pray on the beach. Fresh air and privacy in case you want to talk." Roger led the way.

Ming folded his camp chair, and they trudged across the boardwalk to the beach.

It was peaceful and quiet this Thursday evening. A lukewarm breeze blew across the ocean toward them. All Ming could think of was how he had never invited Sabine to take a beach walk with him. He himself hadn't had time to do so lately. He used to walk in the mornings with his sister in those days past when she had been single and still finishing up her doctorate studies.

Someday when Sabine returned, Ming should do all that with her.

If she returns.

He took a deep breath.

"That's it. Inhale. Exhale." Roger stopped walking. "I'm serious."

"Roger, tell me something."

"What?"

"Are you interested in Sabine?"

"Are you kidding me? She's not my type." Roger unfolded his camp chair. "This is as good a spot as any."

"Not your type?"

"Nope. She's out of focus."

"What do you mean?" Ming set up his camp chair and sat down.

"I was trying to converse with her Tuesday night, right? She kept glancing at you, wherever you might be. She couldn't concentrate on what I was saying. I wasn't starting an intellectual discourse, I tell you. Just making small talk. That's all."

Ming cleared his throat. "She was distracted the entire time?"

"Absolutely. She started every sentence with *Ming*. You know how annoying that is? Ming this. Ming that. Pretty soon your name could become a verb."

"Did you say I'm annoying?"

"That's not what I meant," Roger said. "I mean she's clearly in love with you."

"You think so?"

Roger threw up his arms. "Why would she mention you every time she talked? How else do you define love?"

"I have no idea." But it sure made Ming feel better.

He would feel a whole lot better if his liaisons had—

Ping!

Ming couldn't get to his iPhone fast enough.

He was running before he yelled back at Roger.

"Thanks for praying, man! God is answering our prayers!"

CHAPTER TWENTY-SIX

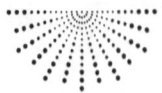

"When this is over and we get out of here, I'm going back to church." Mama Hu rolled over into a supine position in her cage, her legs bent up.

"Good to hear, Mom." About five feet away, Sabine was in her own cage. She figured it was the biggest dog cage made. Perhaps for a Great Dane. Or a Hungarian Komondor. Still, while she could stand up, she couldn't lie down stretched out, unlike her petite mom.

Sabine had taken after Dad, and was taller than both her mom and her sister, but this was a disadvantage for her now. Her legs hurt, as she had to bend them a lot.

Their captors had not allowed them out except to use the bathroom.

She had to find a way to get out of here.

"Do you know of any good church?" Mom asked.

"I've started going to Riverside Chapel."

"Never heard of it."

"Ming's church."

"He never mentioned it to me." Mom faced Sabine. "What's going on with you and Ming?"

"We're friends." There was more, but Sabine wasn't ready to tell Mom.

"Only friends? He seems rather protective of you."

"Is he?" It might be good to hear, but too late. She might never see him again until heaven.

"Yes. Rather defensive when I talked to him about you."

Sabine grimaced as she changed position on the dirty floor in the trailer home. The cage definitely wasn't coming off its bolts. What she wouldn't give for a pillow. "Why does everyone talk about me behind my back?"

"We care for you. Don't want you to get hurt."

"I'm not a baby anymore."

"You'll always be my baby girl, Sabine." Mom's voice broke.

"Mom, don't worry. God will take care of us." Sabine's voice was resolute. "When we make it out of here, we can visit Riverside Chapel together."

"All right. Let's do it. Where is it?"

"On a riverboat by River Street."

Mom cackled. "No kidding? Is the bar open?"

"It's a church on Sundays, Mom."

"Who knows these days what's open. I suppose the slot machines are not available either."

"I didn't see any. I think the casino is closed during the church service."

"But the offering plate is not." Mom had a penchant for sarcasm, but Sabine let it roll off. If talking kept them fighting and kept their hopes up, then Mom could say whatever she wanted.

Lord Jesus, help us.

"And something else." Mom wasn't finished.

"What?"

"I'm changing the name of the company back to Hu Private Investigations, Inc."

"You said it sounded bland. What's wrong with Hu Knows, Inc., Mom?"

"Some people don't take it seriously, dear, as you can see."

"You think they won't put us in cages if you change the name of the firm back?"

Mom didn't have a chance to reply. Sabine heard a panting sound.

It was the mangy golden retriever again, chained to the other end of the double-wide trailer. He was an old dog, but he snarled like he could destroy them.

Sabine prayed again for a way to befriend the golden. She looked down at her paper plate. Yes, she had left half a piece of the stale roll they'd given to her for lunch—or dinner. She pinched half of that and held it up.

"Hey, Pickles. It's just you and us again." Oh, she didn't know whether his name was Pickles. That was what she decided to call him. She kept her voice soft and quiet. "Pickles, for you."

She slid the bread through the steel grids onto the floor outside the cage. She flicked it toward the dog like the bread was a puck from the game of Carrom.

She retreated to the other end of the cage. She fell asleep waiting for Pickles to accept her peace offering.

CHAPTER TWENTY-SEVEN

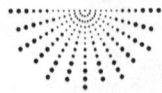

*A*idan Ming Wei body-slammed the bearded man against the alley wall, pressing his head on the exposed brick next to a graffiti-smeared trash bin. In the dim street lights, he couldn't tell how the man was reacting, but he didn't care. This man had mugged Sabine three weeks before.

"Tell me where they are!" Ming screamed into his ears.

Ming had almost lost it when he found out who the SCMPD had released after a brief, fruitless interrogation. Out in the streets, Helen's team had followed this man around town. They had all ended up here shortly after midnight when Ming couldn't keep a lid on it anymore.

"Ming! Stop!" Earl grabbed one arm, and Hugo had Ming's other arm.

They peeled Ming off the poor man, who tried to run, but not before Helen Hu smacked him down to the ground and planted a five-inch stiletto on his chest.

"I'll sue you for police brutality." The man spat something dark from his mouth.

"Except we're not the police, loser," Helen snapped back.

Still, the damage was done. Earl had called his name, and Ming was certain the man remembered it. He hoped the man couldn't identify him with his baseball cap over his hair, but there was no guarantee.

Earl and Hugo kicked the man over and tied his arms behind his back with cable ties. They lifted him up and shoved him into the back of their black van. Earl slammed the door shut after Hugo got in the back with the man.

An anonymous tip that another Hu Knows associate, Gorman, had received said that this man ran errands for Oso the Bear, and all leads started to point to the international fugitive as having something to do with the disappearances of Sabine and Mama Hu.

To make matters worse, several weeks ago, Oso had threatened to go after Helen's family.

Ming wished he had been more vigilant. If he had been, none of this might have happened. Sabine would have been safe.

Would have.

"I'll see y'all soon," Ming said to Earl. "No sleep, food, or drinks. Okay?"

Earl nodded, climbing into the driver's seat.

Sirens came closer and closer until the noise echoed in the alley south of Savannah, but Earl had driven away. Ming watched the van disappear out the other end of the alley as he wiped his bloody knuckles on his vest. The raw skin stung, but he didn't care—

For the wrath of man does not produce the righteousness of God.

James 1:20 popped into his head. Of all the times in the world, he had to find himself recalling that verse right now, in this dark alley after midnight.

Was it Diego's fault for preaching convicting sermons at Riverside Chapel? Well, Ming's old friend had reminded him numerous times that the anger of man could not accomplish the righteousness of God.

Forgive me, Lord.

But I didn't have a choice. He's our only lead.

"What?" Helen asked while she texted as she leaned against her SUV. She was still wearing that jacket with the coffee stain on it.

"After this is over, I'm going to marry your sister," Ming blurted.

"What?" Helen's eyes were still on her iPhone as she opened the door to get into the vehicle.

"Never mind."

It was too late to leave. Sirens shrieked to a stop, and Savannah Chatham Metropolitan Police officers filed into the alley, making shadows on the walls as they ran between the vehicle lights and the darkness beyond.

Detective O'Dell ambled toward them, nodded to Ming, then turned his attention to Helen.

"Helen, oh Helen." O'Dell looked around the otherwise empty alley. "One of these days I'll pin you down."

Helen shrugged. "Or you could be out there looking for my mother and sister."

"We're working on it on all fronts. The FBI, GBI, and SCMPD have teamed up. Can't ask for better cooperation."

As O'Dell was talking, a dark SUV with tinted windows approached the alley.

Someone exited the passenger side. Ming recognized her as a special agent from the FBI satellite office in Savannah, but he could not recall her name.

Ming glanced at his iPhone. He was careful not to let anyone see his knuckles, though the night was getting darker. Still no word from his Interpol contacts.

All he had to do was connect the dots. He was quite sure the abductions were related to their current fugitive manhunt. He wished he had been more vigilant about protecting Sabine since the mugging.

Lord, please keep Sabine safe until we find her—

Oh wait. Please keep her safe even after we find her—

Better yet, find her for us, Lord.

Ming felt confident that God would hear his revised prayer, because he had placed Sabine in God's able hands. He had asked God to find her and keep her safe. Surely God would answer such a prayer.

Everyone knew that Mama Hu was a tough nut. Ming wouldn't be surprised if she were to find a way to get her and Sabine out of wherever they were held prisoner.

As for Sabine, Ming knew now that she wasn't a wallflower, considering the surprise she'd given everyone at the shooting range two weeks before.

Given the situation, she would rise to meet the challenge.

Ming was sure of it. It gave him hope that Sabine would tough it out.

Yep. Helen was loud, but Sabine had quiet strength.

Then again, if Sabine should die—

No.

No!

He checked his iPhone, his heart filled with dread. No news. No leads.

Delight yourself also in the Lord, and He shall give you the desires of your heart.

Ming bowed his head.

God hadn't left his side. Only God would bring to his mind the comfort of Scripture. Only God would bring into his life his good friend, Diego, that walking Bible concordance.

Who would have thought that when Diego reminded him of Psalm 37:4 on Tuesday that Ming would need this verse so soon?

Only God.

What are my desires, Lord?

I want Sabine.

The thought came into his mind just like that. Well, what if God didn't want him to have Sabine for life? What if his relationship with Sabine was only for a couple of months? What if this was the end of it?

What if she died?

Lord Jesus, please, I beg You. No.

Ming lost track of what Helen, O'Dell, and the FBI agent were talking about. They continued to chatter in front of him, but Ming felt at peace now. Whatever they did, only God could take care of the matter.

In his right vest pocket, he fingered Sabine's cross pendant.

I leave Sabine at the foot of Your cross, Lord.

She is Yours first.

So am I. Teach me what it means to delight in You, Lord.

CHAPTER TWENTY-EIGHT

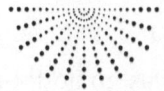

*M*ing shut the door behind him, balancing a bottled water and a doughnut in a napkin in one hand and carrying a folding chair in the other hand. He walked slowly across the windowless room, his boots making soft thuds on the concrete floor. Above him, a dim lightbulb flickered.

"Thirsty?" Ming placed the water and doughnut on the floor directly in front of a chair to which the man was chained. His arms were smeared with blood.

His fingerprints and DNA had matched those of Andre Cornell, forty-two years old, divorced, doing odd jobs here and there, and taking payments in cash only. He had a daughter whom he hadn't seen in four years. His ex-girlfriend had disappeared with her.

There was a lot Ming could work with if he kept his cool.

Earl and Hugo had treated him fairly well, but as instructed, they hadn't given him any food or drinks. By now, some five hours of interrogation later, their captive was no doubt thirsty and hungry.

And sleep deprived.

Ming was too. He was exhausted. He hadn't slept all night, watching the interrogation from the other side of the wall, running searches, and calling favors.

It had paid off. He'd sleep later.

Ming sat down facing Cornell. "I hear Miss Stiletto has been here to see you."

Cornell didn't look up.

"You don't want to mess with her," Ming continued. "Those steel heels make deep puncture wounds. Ask me how I know."

Cornell raised an eyebrow.

"Don't want to be on her bad side, you know." Ming sensed an opening. "She's freaking out because Oso has her mother and sister. Her only family. She'd kill to get them back."

Ming was fishing. He had no concrete proof that Oso was behind this. The SCMPD had to let Cornell go because of the lack of evidence.

But the dots were there. If all went well, Cornell would provide the missing link.

"You know why I care?" Ming continued.

No response.

"Ever been in love, Andre?" Ming dangled a key in front of him. He unlocked one of the chains and freed one of Cornell's hands. Ming handed him the bottled water. "Cold water. Straight from the fridge."

Ming watched Cornell drink.

"Once. Vegas." Cornell's voice was tired, as though he wanted all this to be done.

It played right into Ming's hands. "Kids?"

He already knew that.

"One, though I haven't seen her in a while." Cornell hesitated. "Came home one day, and she was gone with my baby daughter."

"Ghosted, huh?" Ming asked.

"What?"

"Never mind. Point is, she took your baby. Flesh and blood." Ming handed him the chocolate frosted doughnut in the napkin.

Cornell said nothing as he took it with his free hand.

"Oso took my girlfriend, and I want her back." Ming steeled his voice. "Your ex took your daughter, and you want her back."

No response.

"If the Feds get you again—and you know they're at the door—you'll never be able to find your little Paige again."

"How did you..."

"Connections," Ming said. "I'll make a deal with you. You help me find my girlfriend, and I'll help you find your daughter."

Cornell chewed the doughnut slowly.

Ming waited.

"And get Oso off my back?" Cornell asked.

There we go. The dots are connected. "We can arrange that. Oso is wanted everywhere. FBI, Scotland Yard, Interpol."

"That so?"

"Uh-huh." Ming didn't want to be patient, but he had no choice. Cornell was their best lead. "He did tell you to scare my girlfriend a little, right? You knocked her down."

"All I could do—"

Cornell clammed up, but it was too late.

Bingo.

In Ming's vest pocket, his iPhone continued recording their conversation. He wished he had a video of the session.

"So what would it be?" Ming asked. "You get to hear your daughter call you *Daddy* again or what?"

After a little bit, Cornell said, "You got more chocolate doughnuts?"

"Thought you'd never ask."

Within two hours, Ming was on a flight to San José del Cabo by way of Mexico City and Los Cabos. There, at the edge of the Pacific Ocean, Interpol was waiting to assist.

CHAPTER TWENTY-NINE

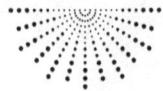

*O*nce a day, Sabine and Mom were let out of their cages to stretch their legs and take a bathroom break, with a giant standing by.

Today, Big Dude didn't look like himself. His pupils were dilated. It was an opportunity for Sabine and Mom to do something, but Sabine was in pain and could hardly stand up. There was no way she was going to be able to run out of here.

Mom was putting on her feisty Mama Hu persona, and Sabine could tell she was plotting their escape.

Sabine crawled out of the cage. Tears made splotches on the grimy floor in front of her. She made her way on her arms and knees to a whining Pickles. The golden retriever had had it worse than she did. He had been beaten again.

Pickles didn't want to be petted.

"It's okay, little one. Does it hurt pretty badly?" Sabine smiled and spoke softly.

The golden lifted an eye at her.

Sabine began to sing, more for herself than the dog. She rolled to her side. She couldn't remember all the words to the hymn, so she made up her own words, calling out to God for mercy and deliverance, begging for heaven.

A spluttery laughter came from Big Dude.

To Sabine's surprise, the dog growled. Then he pointed his doggie nose at Sabine, as if to ask her to continue singing.

Sabine did, though her voice was tired now. She was so famished and starved that all she could think of was heaven. In heaven, the Bible said, there would be feasts and parties with Jesus. All she could eat. All she could drink.

I'll never be hungry or thirsty again.

Mom made a great big show of stretching her legs and arms and moving her neck from side to side. She made some weird noises that sounded like half growls and half moans.

Mom leaned against the built-in table and complained about her sore legs, lawsuits, and other mumbo jumbo she sometimes blathered when she was intoxicated.

Big Dude wasn't impressed.

Mom, you're going to get both of us killed.

Sabine was trying to make faces at her mom to tell her to stop, when something caught her eye. It was metallic and stuck out of a pile of dirt near Mom's feet between the table and the dog.

Sabine stretched as far as she could toward the dog, as if she was trying to pat him.

"I don't think he wants to be petted, woman!" Big Dude barked. "Go ahead and try."

Sabine mustered up all her strength and pushed forward. She spotted it then. A small coil of wire. *Mom could straighten it out—*

She purposely passed Pickles and swiped the coil off the floor. It turned out to be a small torsion spring that someone had dropped. It would have to do.

Sabine retracted her hand toward her mouth and prayed that she could hold the wire in her mouth without poking herself and getting tetanus.

She cooed at Pickles.

Am I seeing things or has he inched toward me?

His paw was out. Sabine slowly pushed her own hand toward the golden. She touched the tip of his paws. He didn't move.

Friends?

"All right! Time to get back into your cages!" Big Dude boomed.

Apparently Sabine was too slow. Big Dude

yanked her up by an arm and dragged her back to her cage. It was then that Sabine noticed an ankle holster peeking out from under the hem of his cargo pants. Above the black Velcro was an outline of a pistol.

"You should thank your lucky stars your ugly legs gross me out, or you and me would have something going." Big Dude kicked Sabine into the cage and slammed the door into her spine. "I wouldn't touch you even if you were the last woman on earth!"

Thank You, Jesus!

"What happened to you, woman?" Big Dude squatted down in front of the cage, as if he was trying to see her face. He spat brown liquid out of his mouth. Tobacco. The drool disgusted Sabine more than his words about her scars. "Did someone dip your legs into a fryer?"

Sabine's forehead was on the floor, her matted hair brushing against the dirt on the linoleum. Little bits of tears caked the dirt.

The smell of male sweat lingered in the stale air around her as Big Dude shuffled away.

A gentle whisper filled her heart with quietude.

Not that I speak in regard to need, for I have learned in whatever state I am, to be content...

She couldn't remember where she had heard it preached before. She had attended numerous churches and heard a number of sermons. Somewhere in the last three years, she had heard a preacher talk about it. Regardless of who had preached it, the verse was from the Word of God, and it never returned void.

Paul, in confinement toward the end of his life, had written a letter to one of the churches in his day. Now Sabine knew what Philippians 4:11 meant. Paul's contentment was in Christ.

In Christ, not in my circumstances.

Thank You, Jesus!

The rattling of chains against a steel cage startled Sabine. She heard Mom yowling and Big Dude mocking her with derogatory words about Asians in general, as he exited the trailer.

Don't respond, Mom. Please don't.

Mom didn't. At least Sabine didn't hear anything from her. All she heard now was the man locking and bolting the trailer door from the outside. Somewhere out there, there were voices too muffled for Sabine to discern.

"Get some sleep, baby girl," Mom said in her calmest voice yet. It meant something was up. "It's going to be a very long night."

Mom has seen what I picked up.

As soon as Sabine couldn't hear any outside

voices or noises anymore, she spat out the steel spring. It looked clean now. Ha!

She lifted her blouse and wiped her tongue on the cotton streaked with dried sweat and dirt from the floor on which she had to sleep.

She picked up the torsion spring. "Mom?"

Mom gave her two thumbs up.

"Give me strength, God." Sabine flicked the metal spring as far as she could.

It skimmed and bounded across the grimy floor and landed a foot short of Mom's cage. "Oh no."

Before she knew it, one of Mom's petite arms reached out all the way to her elbow. She picked up the spring. "Got it. Good work, dear."

Dear?

I've been promoted from baby girl.

CHAPTER THIRTY

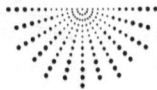

*S*abine was feeling weak from the lack of food. She had been sharing the little she had been given with the old golden retriever. Both of them had been starving, but now neither was going to die.

Prayerfully.

It felt like the middle of the night, but Sabine had no idea what time it was. She had been trying to sleep sitting up. Her tailbone hurt, her legs hurt, her ankles hurt, everything hurt.

But she was alive.

Thank You, Jesus!

She heard Mom's chains clink against the cage steel, and Mom hushing them to be quiet.

Yep. Just like Mom to talk to inanimate objects.

"I'm out, Sabine."

Sabine opened her eyes. In the dim light, she saw Mom put her chains on the floor and shuffle toward Sabine's cage.

"One sec." Mom worked the padlock.

This close, Sabine could see Mom's dirty face. The dirt blocked the black eye Mom had gotten first day in. Sabine remembered seeing it the morning after their abduction. Mom had been abducted first, then Sabine.

Sabine looked past Mom. The golden was awake, alert. He was eyeing them.

Mom picked the lock easily, which made Sabine wonder why they hadn't tried it sooner. She had no idea how long they'd been in there. All the windows were shuttered day and night, and it seemed to be night all the time. Big Dude only came at night. Or was it day?

Chains off, door opened, Sabine was out.

Her legs were flaccid. She hung on to Mom. Her petite Mom was strong, but their movement was slow. At the door, they realized their impossible situation.

The door was locked from the outside.

The windows were all shuttered with metal bars soldered all around.

If there was a fire in here, they'd be burned alive.

Sabine leaned against the wall of the trailer, and prayed.

"We wait for someone to open the door," Mom said.

Sabine sat down on the floor. Pickles came to lick her arm. Sabine worked on his collar and unlatched the leash. "You're coming with us, Pickles."

"Look for sharp objects, Sabine." Mom bounced here, there, everywhere. "Anything not bolted down."

Mom bounced back to where Sabine and the golden were sitting. "You should've taken karate when you were little, Sabine. Your ballet lessons are useless now."

Sabine didn't know whether to laugh or cry. She had taken ballet for the poise. Being a tall, lanky girl in elementary school, she had been awkward on her feet. Ballet had given her gait some balance. Later, it had helped her modeling career.

Sabine wanted to open her mouth to remind Mom that Dad had said a bullet trumped her black belt, but she decided to keep the peace. Mom was stressed. They had to get out.

Lord, give me strength to stand up.

Pins and needles accompanied her as Sabine pulled herself up against the window sill. She heard chains.

"These will have to do." Mom held two long chains in both hands. Those chains looked heavy, but in Sabine's eyes they almost looked like nunchakus or chain whips or something.

Pickles lifted his ears.

"Mom," Sabine warned. She pointed to the golden, now on high alert. "Someone's coming."

"All right. Get behind me, baby girl." Mom moved to one side of the front door where the hinges were. Each of her hands held one end of the chain that used to hang on their cage doors.

Sabine found the light switch near the front door and flicked it off. They were standing in the dark.

Pickles started to growl.

"Shhh..." Sabine stroked his fur.

The trailer door rattled.

Loud voices at the door made Sabine perk up. She heard parts of the conversation outside.

"Move them..."

"Oso says...now... "

Oso? Who is Oso?

Move what now?

Sabine knew a smattering of Spanish, having learned some words and phrases from her friend, Tobias Vega. *Oso* meant bear. What kind of bear? Sabine had no idea.

The door creaked open, and as per usual, only one person stepped in.

Mom leapt up into the air, coiled the chain around Big Dude's neck, and pulled back. He staggered.

Pickles bit his calf.

In the light from outside—moonlight!—Sabine was able to see his khaki pants. She squatted down and yanked the pistol from his ankle holster. Big Dude kicked her, his boots making contact with her chest, and she fell back.

He pushed back, pinning Mom to the wall. She was screaming, trying to get air. Her hands were loosening around the chains.

Sliding to a stop, Sabine was lying on her back, facing up. The safety off on the pistol, she pointed the weapon at Big Dude. "Let her go."

Big Dude chortled and made a bad move. He elbowed Mom, who was still pinned to the wall behind him. Mom collapsed. She didn't move.

"Mom!" Sabine's hands were shaking so badly she didn't have the strength to pull the trigger.

We're going to die.

Bid Dude lurched.

"Don't move," Sabine snapped. She couldn't move herself. Still on the ground, she couldn't feel her legs. They'd gone numb on her.

Help me, Jesus!

"Are you stupid, woman? My guys outside have shotguns. You have nothing."

Sure enough, she could hear shots fired outside. Lots of noise.

Sabine's lips quivered. She kept the pistol pointed at Big Dude. "You move, and I'm going to...to..."

Yep, we're dead.

"To what? Tell me." He stepped forward.

Sabine pulled the trigger.

It was an awful sound to see Big Dude drop to the floor and hear him scream like a little girl so loudly Sabine thought her eardrums were going to blow out.

Pickles came to her side and sat down on the floor next to her.

"Good boy." Sabine kept her eyes on Big Dude, who was trying to get up. "Stop!"

"Or you'll what?" Big Dude shuffled on his bottom. One of his legs was bleeding.

Sabine prayed she hadn't nicked his artery.

There was fury in Big Dude's eyes. "I dare you to shoot me again, you—"

The door fell in. Crashed right next to Big Dude.

Click.

"You'd better do what she said, whatever it was."

Ming!

Sabine blinked. "Is that really you?"

"It's me." That silly grin. "Now which one of you screamed so loudly we heard it across the trailer park?"

Ming's Glock was on Big Dude's forehead.

Around them, Helen was jumping around, prancing, screeching. "Mom! Sabine! You okay? Mom!"

Yep, Helen's excited.

Swarming all around them were law enforcement officers in Kevlar vests and helmets. When one of the officers' backs faced Sabine, she saw three letters that brought so much relief to her she began to cry.

FBI.

Several other men and women surrounded them, and on their sleeves were the word POLICE.

"We'll take it from here, Mr. Wei," one of them said.

"Glad you came just in time." Ming holstered his Glock, the same one that Sabine had borrowed at the River Run Indoor Range the other day.

He rushed to Sabine, quietly removed the pistol from her hand, and handed it to an officer nearby. "The SWAT and FBI will take over, okay?"

Sabine nodded.

"Thank God you're all right," Ming said. "Hurting anywhere?"

Sabine gasped. "Pins and needles in my legs."

He massaged them.

Across the small trailer, the paramedics worked on Mom and carried her out on a stretcher.

"Is Mom okay?" Sabine asked.

One of the paramedics nodded.

And no, Sabine didn't want any help. She tried to get up. She limped a little. She closed her eyes and prayed.

Thank You, Jesus.

Pickles licked her arm.

"I'm rescuing this golden," Sabine announced to Ming. "His name is Pickles. Come on, Pickles. Let's go home."

"Okay." Ming looked down at the dog. Pickles wagged his tail. "I guess I could live with that."

Sabine hobbled, Pickles by her side. She didn't go very far.

Ming slid his arms around Sabine and gently scooped her up. She wrapped her arms around Ming's neck and wept softly as he carried her out to an awaiting stretcher right outside the trailer door.

Mom was in another stretcher ,with Helen holding her hand. "Sabine."

"Mom." Sabine stretched out her arm toward Mom as they strapped her onto the stretcher.

Mother and daughters held hands. Helen was softly crying.

"Helen, we're fine," Sabine said. "God took care of us."

Helen nodded. "God is good."

"All the time," Sabine added.

"And all the time, God is good," Mom concluded. "Heard that somewhere."

"It's true." Sabine smiled.

Looking up into the clear night sky as she was wheeled to the ambulance, Sabine spotted the Orion constellation. A light airplane skittered overhead. Stars began to twinkle.

What a beautiful night.

Thank You, Jesus.

CHAPTER THIRTY-ONE

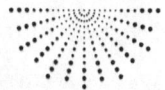

S abine opened her eyes to dim light and someone holding her hand. She felt the soft sheets under her. She knew exactly what a hospital mattress felt like.

Oh no. I'm back in the hospital again.

Her entire body felt sore, but she could move both legs.

Thank You, Jesus.

Even if she couldn't move her legs, she would still be content with the days—many or few—that God allowed her to have. That, she had learned while being locked up in a cage for a week.

She had no doubt about God's love, but what about Ming's love? "Is it possible for you to love me anymore?"

"It's not possible for me to love you any less."

Ming sat closer to Sabine on the bed. He lifted her hand to his lips. "Marry me, Sabine. Marry me now. Today. We can ask the chaplain to officiate. I saw him down the hallway just now."

"What about premarital counseling? I want to talk to Pastor Flores first."

"What for? We're not marrying him. Besides, his sessions take six weeks. I can't wait six weeks."

"Love is patient, love is kind..."

"Love is now."

"That's not in the Bible, Ming."

"All right. If you want to wait six weeks, we can wait six weeks."

"Maybe we could ask for double sessions."

"Then we'll be done in three weeks." Ming's face brightened up.

Sabine shifted in the bed. She flinched, but the pain eased quickly. "Either way, we're looking at April."

Ming helped her with her blanket. "We can be married among the daffodils in my backyard."

"Daffodils? You have daffodils?" Sabine didn't remember Ming ever mentioning daffodils. She tried to recall their times together since February when they first started working together to sell his house. Nope. Not a word about daffodils.

"Yep. In the springtime. Oh, it's not my house any more."

"Right. We'll have to ask your sister and brother-in-law about *their* backyard."

"We? So you said yes?"

"What's the question?"

"I'll die if you don't marry me."

"No, you won't."

"Just trying to make my point. Marry me, Sabine. I want to wake up every morning with you by my side. I want us to grow old together, sit in rocking chairs watching the sun rise every morning, and take long walks on the beach with our coffee mugs in tow."

"Sounds lovely."

"I want to love you and be loved by you until we're a hundred years old or more."

To love and be loved.

Sabine couldn't speak.

Ming wiped away the tears from her face with the tips of his fingers.

He leaned down toward her ear. "I love you, Sabine. I love, love, love you. I've loved you since—I can't remember when—February, I guess."

Sabine laughed. Sure was a whirlwind.

Ming sat up. "Did I tell you I love you?"

"Multiple times. I don't mind." Sabine smiled.

"Better not mind. I'll tell you that the rest of my life."

"What about Pickles?" Sabine asked.

"Nobody claimed him. The neighbors said that his old owner had died recently. The new owner of the trailer continued to keep him there. You know his name used to be Bob."

"He doesn't look like Bob. I'm calling him Pickles." Sabine wanted to sit up.

Ming put up a palm. "The neighbors are all happy he's going to a good home and not to the pound."

"Where is he now?" Sabine asked.

"At Helen's house until you can take him home." Ming rubbed Sabine's hand. "She took him to the vet this morning, or at least her assistant did. You know he's about nine years old. Goldens don't live long."

"I want to care for him the rest of his life. He'll have a few happy years with me." Sabine sniffed. "It's too bad you sold your house."

"Why?"

"Pickles would love that yard, I think."

"We'll buy another house with plenty of room for a dog." Ming paused. "And kids."

"One step at a time." Sabine thanked God for Ming. Their separation had been brief but profound. She had learned to be contented in her circumstances.

Even if she couldn't walk again, even if she had scars everywhere on her legs, she was alive.

Alive and well.

Alive in Christ.

I am content in You, Lord Jesus. Thank You.

"I love you, Ming," Sabine said quietly. "I can't believe I'm in the hospital again."

"You'll heal. And you're being discharged this afternoon."

"Thank God."

"At least nothing's broken, you know, like last time. This time it's just a twisted ankle. That's all. I'll be carrying you over the threshold after our wedding anyway, so it doesn't matter if you couldn't walk, though we know you will. No worries. Besides, I get to pamper you and grill you my famous salmon burg—"

Sabine grabbed Ming's tee shirt and pulled him down toward her. "The answer is yes."

Ming's face showed a faint trace of something mischievous. "The pampering or the wedding?"

"Everything." And she kissed him just as Mom and Helen burst into the room carrying bouquets of flowers.

CHAPTER THIRTY-TWO

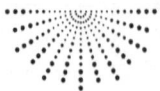

*M*ing had insisted that he and Sabine marry the morning after their last premarital counseling session. As soon as the counseling session had ended on a cloudy Friday afternoon, it rained heavily the entire evening and all through the night.

The rain had ruined any hope of a sunrise wedding in the muddy backyard. The April wedding would now take place inside Ming's old house—and Heidi's new one.

Ming had been disappointed until he remembered that he was supposed to delight himself in the Lord, not in fickle weather patterns.

Well, indoor wedding is fine as long as we're married!

Ming paced up and down the newly renovated

living room and sunroom. The folding doors had been pushed back, and the entire space looked like a little chapel, with sunlight filtering through the stained-glass transom windows in the sunroom, shining down on rows of fabric-covered wedding chairs lined up all the way to the walls separating the living room and the Floreses' bedrooms.

Ming glanced incessantly at the clock on his iPhone, when shrieks and screams startled him.

He jumped as Pickles the golden retriever ran past him, his doggie bow tie askew, his entire body from nose to tail wet and covered with mud.

Ming freaked out. "Who let the dog out?"

Ming chased Pickles, who bolted into the sunroom. He screeched to a halt on the aisle and wildly shook his body, splattering brown mud, dirty rain water, and the great backyard on the white chiffon wedding chair covers, the oak floor, on Ming's tuxedo pants, and everywhere.

Ming's arms reached for the dog's neck—uh, collar.

Pickles dropped to the ground. His sad, round eyes gazed up at Ming. He made pathetic whining sounds. Then he rolled over to have his tummy rubbed.

Ming stared in disbelief.

Then he laughed.

He rubbed Pickles's stomach, cooing sweet

gibberish to the poor dog. "How can anyone be mad at you? You've had a long, hard life."

Ming took a deep breath, closed his eyes, and prayed to God for mercy.

Then he took off his tuxedo jacket and threw it on a clean chair. He clapped his hands and raised his voice.

"Listen up, everyone. I need mops, lots of rags, and a designated dog handler. We're going to clean up this mess in"—he stared at his iPhone—"thirty minutes. Can we do it so Sabine and I can get married pronto?"

~

Sabine tossed the bouquet of light-pink roses in sprays of white baby's breath. The pretty arrangement sailed through the air into the crowd of ladies on the deck, some with arms outstretched, some amused, and some not participating at all.

Not Sabine's sister.

Helen launched into the air in her sea-blue bridesmaid gown and intercepted the bouquet in an acrobatic style as graceful as a duck leaping into the air. All the single Hu and Wei cousins converged upon her as if to demonstrate a rugby tackle.

Sabine's eyes widened as she hid a grin behind her gloved hand.

Ming slid his arms around her and locked his fingers together on her waist, against her embroidered wedding gown.

"Ready to go?" he whispered.

"One sec."

"Okay. I'll wait by the front door." Ming looked sharp in his tuxedo.

Sabine walked through the crowd, milling. All the guests had helped to move the wedding chairs around so they could turn the space into a reception area.

Diego and Heidi Flores, proud new owners of the house, were offering the guests more wedding cupcakes from trays.

Sabine passed by the happy couple and found Pickles in the kitchen. chewing on a bone.

She squatted down and patted Pickles's head. "We'll be back in three days to pick you up, okay?"

Pickles wagged his tail, but clearly his focus was on the bone. In the sunlight through the kitchen windows, his fur was now shiny, clean, and oddly damp. It smelled like fresh shampoo.

Who gave Pickles another bath? Why?

Sabine frowned when he saw specks of mud on Pickles's bow tie. She tugged at it. "So what happened here?"

Pickles didn't respond.

Sabine heard footsteps coming into the kitchen.

"We'll try not to overfeed him," a woman's voice said.

Sabine turned to see Heidi placing an empty tray on the island. "I saved two cupcakes for you on the road."

"You're thoughtful."

"Least I can do since the rest will be eaten."

Sabine glanced over at the front door beyond the living room where Ming was gesturing to her. Hurry up, he seemed to say.

"We'll be back soon," Sabine said. "But you can call us anytime if Pickles needs us."

"Like Ming always says, no worries," Heidi said.

CHAPTER THIRTY-THREE

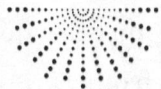

"*D*o you think Pickles will be okay?" Sabine asked as Ming drove the SUV on Butler Avenue heading north toward the Tybee Island Light Station and Highway 80 heading for downtown Savannah. "He was pulling at the leash when we drove away."

"No worries, Sabine," Ming said. "We'll only be gone for a few days."

"He could forget us." Sabine wished they could have taken Pickles with them, but it would be unusual. The golden was better off playing in Heidi's yard than being stuck in a crate in the airplane with the newlyweds.

"He'll remember," Ming assured her. "Wait and see."

Still... Something bugged Sabine. She couldn't put a finger on it.

Lord Jesus, what is it?

"What's on your mind, Sabine?" Ming asked.

"I don't know. Lots of stuff, I guess."

"Don't be nervous. We're husband and wife now. My sister said that married people should be transparent with each other."

It'll take time. Sabine looked out the window of her SUV. Ming was a good driver; the ride was smooth.

Just before they crossed over Chimney Creek, Sabine saw the sign.

"Stop. Stop!" She tapped Ming's right shoulder.

"What?" Ming slowed down.

"Could you turn back? I need to see something on a side road there."

"The one we just passed? Left or right?"

"Right side coming this way." Sabine was happy that Ming was accommodating. "There's a house for sale. See the red sign?"

"Should've guessed." Ming shook his head. "May I remind you we have a plane to catch?"

"We have several hours, remember?"

They had planned on stopping at Sabine's penthouse to pack, then having a lunch date at Belford's before they flew out to their free villa in San José del

Cabo. Their flight wasn't until after two in the afternoon.

So what's the rush? "Let's have a look."

Ming breathed in deeply. "How much is this going to cost us?"

"Park and I'll find out." Sabine was on her iPhone, checking her go-to real estate website for pricing information as Ming flicked on the blinker to make a U-turn.

Sabine pointed. "That road across the street. There. Third house down."

Ming drove slowly. "Surprise, surprise. It has a rooftop deck. Nestled among the trees."

"It has a pool house next to a lap pool. Fenced yard. Half an acre," Sabine read off her iPhone. "Short sale."

"Short sale, huh? Well, if my business revives..."

"I'll sell my condo," Sabine blurted. "This house is priced at a hundred thou under. We'll have money left over."

"Never too early to save for college and retirement." Ming cleared his throat.

"Or invest in business."

"Business? You mean you'd like to expand your real estate agency and interior designing business?"

"Or if you happen to know of a fledgling PI firm in need of financial backing..."

"Hmmm... I might." Ming's lips curled into a...

Frown.

It threw off Sabine.

Then Ming said, "I thought you liked your penthouse."

"It was great when I lived alone. But we're married now. We talked about getting a house for us and a yard for Pickles to run around. I don't want him falling off a rooftop terrace chasing after a tennis ball."

"Can't have that, can we? Not just dogs, but our kids—future kids—could also fall off the roof." Ming coasted to a stop in the driveway. "Before we do anything, let's be sure we know what we're doing."

"Love your cool head, Ming." Sabine held his hand. "Let's pray."

"Good idea." Ming closed his eyes, and they prayed for godly counsel and the right timing.

Sabine climbed out of the car. "Let's look at the house, shall we?"

"Sure, if we don't miss our flight." Ming followed Sabine up the driveway. To one side was a well-landscaped garden.

"Look there, Ming. Azaleas. Daffodils. Tulips along the wooden fence."

"Hmmm... I could be persuaded since this garden is ready to go. I'll only need to maintain it." Ming held her hand as they stood there. "It's not on the beach though. I thought we wanted an ocean view."

"One sec." Sabine was on her iPhone again. "There's a private path to the beach."

"That'll do."

Sabine stepped closer to Ming. "Oh, look at us. Did you realize—never mind."

She was still in her wedding gown, veil off.

Ming had removed his tuxedo jacket and bow tie.

"Well, we don't care, do we?" Ming smiled. "If you want to see this house, let's go see this house, and we'll be on our way. Can you get the key?"

Sabine checked her iPhone again and obtained the lockbox number. It was one of the perks of being a real estate agent. She opened the lockbox to retrieve the key.

Before they unlocked the house, Sabine turned to Ming and said, "This could be one of many houses we look at, but one of these beauties could be our home."

"Home? Home is with you." Ming lifted her chin. "I know what you're doing. You're stalling because we're heading to our honeymoon villa. We'll be there tonight, our wedding night. You must be nervous."

"I'm not—"

"It's me, Sabine." Ming stroked her arms gently.

"I don't see what you think I see. I only see my beautiful bride, the love of my life, the blessing from God."

Sabine sniffled.

"Hey." He hugged her and kissed her forehead. "Want to know something?"

Sabine tilted her head, waiting, wondering what Ming was about to say.

"Sabine, love of my life, I believe that nothing I have ever gone through, none of those stab wounds, gunshot wounds, rounds of disfiguring surgeries, and whatever else, can compare with what Jesus Christ went through on the cross, dying in shame for me."

"Me too."

"Then what's the problem?" Ming asked.

"I don't want you to see..." She couldn't say it.

"Is there anything in this world that can ever compare to the scars on our Savior's hands and feet?"

Scars.

Sabine opened her mouth to speak, but nothing came out.

Ming wasn't done. "I'm your husband now, and hopefully the only one the rest of your life. Your scars are mine, and mine are yours."

Your scars are mine, and mine are yours.

Sabine buried her face in his neck so that he couldn't see her tears.

Ming rubbed her back. "Genesis 2:24 says, 'Therefore a man shall leave his father and mother and be joined to his wife, and they shall become one flesh.' One flesh, Sabine."

Sabine pulled away and saw the Bible app on the iPhone in Ming's hand. "Ha. Here I was, thinking you had memorized the verse. Sneaky."

Ming grinned as he tucked away his phone. "In my own defense, I did read Genesis 2:24 this morning for my daily devotional."

Sabine nodded. She had read something else in her devotional, but she couldn't remember exactly which verse in Ephesians 5.

Well, it looked like she would have to read it again.

She had been wondering what God wanted her to learn on her wedding day.

Something Ming had said...

Your scars are mine, and mine are yours.

One flesh.

Husband and wife.

Sabine closed her eyes.

Thank You, Jesus.

"If you still want to look at houses for sale on the way to our honeymoon, that's okay by me, as long as I'm with you." Ming planted kisses on her neck and ears and lips. "Now that we're married, I suppose we have all the time in the world."

"All the time in the world for what?" Sabine asked. "I guess you'll tell me soon."

"I'll tell you now, Mrs. Wei." And he whispered in her ear.

Sabine blushed. "In that case, I guess the house tours can wait."

～

DEAR READER:

I hope you enjoyed the story of Sabine and Ming. While *Tell You Soon* is a beach romance with elements of suspense, the next book in the Savannah Sweethearts series, *Draw You Near*, is an international romance with a backdrop of water-colors and landscape paintings. Check out this coastal romance between an American artist and a handsome British tourist.

Draw You Near (Savannah Sweethearts Book 4)
JanThompson.com/draw

Read the Sequel

Ming and Sabine return together for a sequel in a Christian Romantic Suspense novel, *Once Bitten, Twice Shy* (Guardian Sweethearts Book 1). This novel, in turn, is the prequel to *Once a Thief* (Protector Sweethearts Book 1).

Once Bitten, Twice Shy (Guardian Sweethearts
Book 1)
JanThompson.com/shy
Once a Thief (Protector Sweethearts Book 1)
JanThompson.com/thief

READ A FREE EBOOK!

Set in Georgia, South Carolina, and Tennessee, this Christian romance tells the story of art gallery archivist Sheryl Breckenridge and world-famous sculptor Winton Pace.

Time for Me (A Vacation Sweethearts Prequel)
JanThompson.com/time-free

JOIN MY BOOK NEWS MAILING LIST

Subscribe to my mailing list to receive updates on the books that I have written, am writing, and will be writing. You don't want to miss surprise book sales and special announcements. Be the first to know about my new book releases.

Jan Thompson's Book News Mailing List:
JanThompson.com/newsletter

PLEASE WRITE A REVIEW

Thank you for reading *Tell You Soon*. If you'd like to leave a review, please follow the link below to find the retailers that carry this ebook.

Tell You Soon (Savannah Sweethearts Book 3)
JanThompson.com/tell

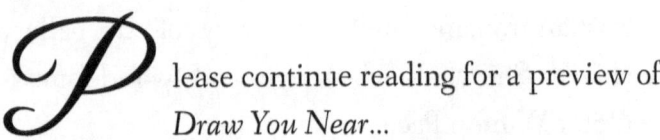

lease continue reading for a preview of *Draw You Near...*

THE NEXT BOOK IS DRAW YOU NEAR

SAVANNAH SWEETHEARTS BOOK 4

*Lars and Abilene are drawn to each other,
but will their relationship end up
like an unfinished painting?*

Savannah artist Abilene Dupree keeps her personal life out of her commercial paintings except one. That one painting has now brought Londoner Lars Tabansi Cargill back to the coastal town and into her art world.

Can she hold him at bay before he invades her personal space and paints his way into her heart?

LARS'S LABOR...

While on vacation in Savannah last year, Lars Cargill bought a small watercolor painting for his estate in England. The more he stared at the artwork, the more he wanted to meet the woman in the painting.

This summer, Lars returns to Savannah to find the elusive real-life Lady and the Sea. Problem is, the artist says she doesn't exist.

Of course, he doesn't believe her. Otherwise, he wouldn't be showing up in her art classes and following her around. He doubts she has the heart to turn him away, not when he shows her that he has artistic potential.

ABILENE'S ART...

Abilene Dupree is busy trying to make a living as an artist and art teacher in Savannah.

She sells commercial art, not personal stories. Although much of her heart goes into her paintings, she doesn't reveal her soul, not even to the clean-cut guy with cute dimples who is searching for the woman in her Lady and the Sea painting.

She keeps telling Lars that the elusive and illusive woman in the painting doesn't exist.

Well, the more she tells him that, the more she begins to believe her own words.

Before she can give him the real answers he seeks, Lars's own past shows up and he has to leave Savannah.

Lars and Abilene are drawn to each other, but will their relationship end up like an unfinished painting?

Draw You Near (Savannah Sweethearts Book 4):
JanThompson.com/draw

Savannah Sweethearts:
JanThompson.com/savannah

To receive publication news about the Savannah Sweethearts series, sign up to be on Jan's mailing list: JanThompson.com/newsletter

DRAW YOU NEAR CHAPTER 1
SNEAK PEEK

*S*unrise was Abilene Dupree's favorite morning hour at the Savannah waterfront.

With River Street still deserted behind her, the Savannah River uncrowded in front of her save for a tall ship and a couple of riverboats, she had a clear view of the May sunrise coming across the sky to her right, casting golden hues on the Talmadge Memorial Bridge to her left, spanning the river to Hutchinson Island on the other side.

Abilene strolled along the river, her easel backpack slung over her shoulders and her oil-paper carrier hanging over an arm, as she sipped hot Starbucks in a ceramic travel mug that an ex-boyfriend had personalized for her.

Past the Rousakis Riverfront Plaza, the second riverboat waited for Abilene. It was smaller than the other.

She found a spot where the morning sun would shine on the riverboat when she painted. She put down her mug and set up her easel.

The dry paper clipped into place, she picked through her tubes of paint, squeezing them onto her palette while humming a hymn from the church service the Sunday before.

Around her, joggers and walkers went about their quiet business. Some tourists stopped to watch Abilene paint.

She was used to it. She just smiled for the camera, waved, and went back to work. Southern charm and all that.

Sure, she was a transplant from New Orleans, but she'd considered Savannah her home for the past ten years.

She was thanking God for the beautiful day that

the Lord had made, when something between her easel and the riverboat caught her eye.

A vision in blue.

Blue shirt, blue cargo shorts.

Oh no.

He walked toward her, two paper cups in his hands. He was tall and fit and buff, but unwelcomed.

"Good morning!"

His British voice, tinged with a faint accent of some sort, was pleasant, she'd give him that.

"You again." Abilene frowned. She'd been frowning all week whenever Lars Tabansi Cargill showed up.

"Me again." The more he smiled, the more his dimples deepened.

His short hair combed down and wet said that he had just gotten out of the shower. But his five o'clock shadow said he hadn't bothered to shave.

Abilene knew Lars was staying at a hotel here on River Street, because he'd told her. He had also told her many other things she didn't want to hear and had asked her questions she didn't want to answer.

"I brought coffee." He offered her one of the cups.

"No, thanks." She pointed to her travel mug on the ground. "I have my own."

"But this is hazelnut, your favorite, isn't it?"

"Not today." He knew too much about her since their first conversation at Simon's Gallery.

A visitor in town, Lars had been pestering her for a week to reveal the identity of the woman in the painting he'd bought from Simon's Gallery a year before.

He had come all the way here from London just to find her. Not Abilene the painter, but the woman in her painting, sitting on a beach chair on Tybee Island.

Abilene remembered that watercolor painting vividly, but she didn't want to talk about it.

"I thought you went home." She dabbed her brush into more paint. She kept moving the brush, hoping that if she looked busy, he'd go away.

"What's another week?" Lars stepped closer.

"Don't you have to work?"

"I'm in between jobs."

"In other words, you're unemployed."

"Self-employed." He fished for a piece of paper from his pocket. Unfolded it.

Abilene rolled her eyes. "No."

"Yes. I need a name." Lars held the paper up. It was a color copy of the painting that had besotted the Londoner. "Give me a name, and I'll be out of your hair."

That was the thing! Lars wanted her to tell him

the history of the painting. She wanted him to be history. "Go home, Lars. There's nothing to tell."

"I'll pay you anything. I want to meet this woman."

"It's just a painting, Lars. Nothing more." Not for him to know, anyway.

"I don't believe you."

"Yeah, you said that last week."

"I asked Simon. He doesn't know."

"No, he doesn't. He just shows my artwork."

Lars opened his mouth to speak just as his phone rang.

"Here, hold this." He handed Abilene one of the coffee cups. "Better drink it before it gets cold."

~

"When are you coming home, Lars?"

"Are you checking up on me?" Lars walked briskly away from Abilene and hoped she couldn't hear the conversation. Somehow he found himself heading toward the riverboat she was painting.

"Have you thought about my proposal?"

"Well, still thinking about it." Not really. Truth be told, Lars wasn't sure he wanted to work at Cargill Internet Communications, family business or not. It seemed dull and uninspiring.

"How long are you going to be in America?" Colm pressed.

"Maybe through the summer. Why?"

"Just wondering."

In his heart, Lars felt good that his brother called. They hadn't spoken in over a week. However, he wondered if Colm would understand what he was doing in Savannah. He would probably call it a silly phase.

Lars stopped at the foot of the ramp leading up to the riverboat. He faced a stand with a clear acrylic box attached. On the box were the words *Riverside Chapel*. Inside were flyers with pictures of the riverboat. The flyers looked somewhat familiar.

He glanced behind his shoulder to find Abilene in the distance waving for him to step aside. He waved back but didn't move. He doubted he was really getting in her way. Well, she could paint around him.

"Summer is a long time, Lars." Colm's voice was deeper than Lars's, but if they were standing side by side, they could pass for fraternal twins.

Only fourteen months apart, they had been inseparable until they went off to different universities. While Colm had chosen to stay closer to home, Lars had gone off to Yale instead. So much for all that money spent. He hadn't done a thing with his MBA.

"You don't need me, Colm." His brother's Oxford degree had served the Cargill empire well.

"No, but since Mom passed away, you're my responsibility."

"Nope, Colm. I can take care of myself."

"Sure. Pushing thirty and not being certain of what you want to do with the rest of your life."

"That's why I'm here. I'm figuring it out."

"In Savannah."

"Yes."

"And it'll take all summer."

"Yes."

Silence.

Lars wondered what Colm was thinking over there in his glass tower.

Still standing in front of the information box, Lars opened the lid and picked up a flyer.

Yep. It was her handiwork. Lars would recognize it anywhere.

Even as he stared at the flyer, his conversation with his brother continued to play in his mind.

"Can't just live off your trust fund, you know."

"Right."

"Can't drift, Lars. You need an anchor."

An anchor? Sure. I'll find an anchor.

Staring at the flyer, Lars decided he would go to church.

Draw You Near (Savannah Sweethearts Book 4):
JanThompson.com/draw

More Information about Savannah Sweethearts:
JanThompson.com/savannah

To keep up with Jan Thompson and her book news:
JanThompson.com/newsletter

READ A FREE EBOOK IN THE SAME STORY WORLD

Set in Georgia, South Carolina, and Tennessee, this clean and wholesome Christian romance tells the story of art gallery archivist Sheryl Breckenridge and world-famous sculptor Winton Pace. Read this ebook for free!

Time for Me (A Vacation Sweethearts Prequel)

JanThompson.com/time-free

ACKNOWLEDGMENTS

Many thanks to my Georgia Press publishing team for keeping up with my writing schedule.

I appreciate author Heather Day Gilbert for copyediting this book, and copyeditor Dori Harrell and proofreader Lenda Selph for proofreading it. Thank you, ladies!

Thank you to EMT Jerrid Edgington for answering my questions about paramedics.

I am grateful to God for my husband and son for their support and encouragement. I also thank God for my parents and my three brothers for my happy and memorable childhood. I'll always remember my beloved mother and my late father for having instilled in me the love of reading and writing from a very early age. I miss my father here on earth, but I will see him again in heaven someday.

Most of all, I am eternally thankful to my Lord and Savior, Jesus Christ, who died on the cross to save me from my sins and rose again from the grave to give me eternal life. Without Him, I can write nothing (John 15:5).

Jan Thompson
John 3:16

BOOKS BY JAN THOMPSON

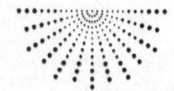

CHRISTIAN BEACH AND ISLAND ROMANCE

Seaside Chapel (7 Books)
  JanThompson.com/seaside
  Journeys of Love through Life's Ups & Downs

CHRISTIAN COASTAL ROMANCE IN THE SOUTH

Savannah Sweethearts (12 Books)
  JanThompson.com/savannah

CHRISTIAN TRAVEL ROMANCE

Vacation Sweethearts (8 Books)
  JanThompson.com/vacation

CHRISTIAN CHRISTMAS ROMANCE IN THE CITY

Midtown Christmas (4 Books)
  JanThompson.com/christmas

CHRISTIAN CHRISTMAS ROMANCE ON THE COAST

Christmas Sweethearts (3 Books)
  JanThompson.com/christmastown

INTERNATIONAL CHRISTIAN ROMANTIC SUSPENSE

Protector Sweethearts (6 Books)
  JanThompson.com/protector
  Treasures Lost and Found

Defender Sweethearts (6 Books)
  JanThompson.com/defender
  Defending the Defenseless Worldwide

PROTECTOR SWEETHEARTS

Private investigator Helen Hu and her associates specialize in searching for missing persons and hunting for lost treasures. Join them in their adventure suspense around the world in *USA Today* bestselling author Jan Thompson's Protector Sweethearts, a series of Christian Romantic Suspense with a side of mystery.

Protector Sweethearts is a spin-off of Savannah Sweethearts and Vacation Sweethearts.

JanThompson.com/protector

- Book 1: *Once a Thief*

- Book 2: *Once a Hero*
- Book 3: *Once a Spy*
- Book 4: *Twice a Fighter*
- Book 5: *Twice a Convict*
- Book 6: *Twice a Soldier*

DEFENDER SWEETHEARTS

Defender Sweethearts is a sister series to the Protector Sweethearts Christian romantic suspense collection. While the heroes in Protector Sweethearts search for lost treasures and lost people, the Defender Sweethearts novels focus on protecting the helpless and hopeless. The main characters in Defender Sweethearts come from the supporting cast in Protector Sweethearts.

JanThompson.com/defender

- Book 1: *Never a Traitor*
- Book 2: *Never a Hostage*

- Book 3: *Never a Fugitive*
- Book 4: *Always a Maverick*
- Book 5: *Always a Champion*
- Book 6: *Always a Guardian*

BINARY HACKERS

Like more suspense with your Christian romance? Like to read suspense thrillers? If you're looking for clean near-future romantic suspense without compromising the Christian faith, these books are for you.

From *USA Today* bestselling author Jan Thompson come these inspirational near-future cyberthrillers combining technothriller and romance, starting with Binary Hackers that feature computer specialists living at the edge of cyber-space, where they have to juggle being law-abiding truth-telling Christians while carrying out their assignments by any and all means possible.

The Binary Hackers series is set in the same story world as Jan's other books, and characters from the other series may make cameo appearances in this series and vice versa.

JanThompson.com/binary

- Book 1: *Zero Sum*
- Book 2: *Zero Day*
- Book 3: *Zero Out*
- Book 4: *Zero Trust*

SEASIDE CHAPEL

Welcome to *USA Today* bestselling author Jan Thompson's Seaside Chapel Christian beach romance series. These novels are set on real-life St. Simon's Island, Georgia—a beach town where history is all around and the future is a moment away—and the neighboring fictitious Seaside Island, where the rich and famous live.

Savor the small-town atmosphere and the warm southern beaches of St. Simon's Island and the idyllic Golden Isles along the Atlantic Ocean. Enjoy the music of the orchestra and hymns of the church, and hang out with our Christian friends who attend Seaside Chapel, a little church by the sea known for its beach weddings and fair share of love and life.

As these Christians grow in their knowledge and understanding of God, they are tested in their spiritual maturity, their love lives, and their relationships with others. Share their heartaches and healing, and cheer them on as they celebrate faith, family, and friends.

JanThompson.com/seaside

- Book 0 (Prequel): *His Surprise Proposal*
- Book 1: *His Longing Heart*
- Book 2: *His Wake-Up Call*
- Book 3: *His Morning Kiss*
- Book 4: *His Quiet Serenade*
- Book 5: *His Waiting Love*
- Book 6: *His Beach Retreat*

SAVANNAH SWEETHEARTS

Welcome to the new south! From *USA Today* bestselling author Jan Thompson come these clean and wholesome, sweet and inspirational Christian romances set on the romantic beaches of Tybee Island and in the coastal town of Savannah, Georgia. Meet a group of multiracial and multiethnic churchgoing Christians who love the Lord, work hard in their careers, and seek God's will for their love lives. Against a backdrop of ocean, sand, and sun, these inspirational romances showcase aspects of the human need for God and for one another. Have some tea, settle in a comfortable reading chair, and enjoy these sweet celebrations of faith, hope, and love in Jesus Christ.

JanThompson.com/savannah

- Book 1: *Ask You Later* (Artist Romance)
- Book 2: *Know You More* (Multiracial Romance)
- Book 3: *Tell You Soon* (Asian-American Romance with Suspense)
- Book 4: *Draw You Near* (International Romance)
- Book 5: *Cherish You So* (Wheelchair Billionaire Romance)
- Book 6: *Walk You There* (Old-Meets-New Tour Guide Romance)
- Book 7: *Love You Always* (Romance with Suspense)
- Book 8: *Kiss You Now* (Multiracial Romance)
- Book 9: *Find You Again* (Multiracial Romance)
- Book 10: *Wish You Joy* (Christmas-Themed Romance)
- Book 11: *Call You Home* (Deaf Chef Romance)
- Book 12: *Let You Go* (Asian-American Romance with Suspense)

VACATION SWEETHEARTS

Travel with our friends from Savannah, Georgia, to the coast and to the mountains. Cheer them on as they celebrate the immeasurable grace and undeserved mercy of God through Jesus Christ.

The Vacation Sweethearts novels are a spin-off of Jan's Savannah Sweethearts series, and fans will recognize familiar faces from Riverside Chapel, a church in the coastal city of Savannah, Georgia. In fact, we might even visit the beach town of Tybee Island from time to time to visit old friends and beloved families...

~

JanThompson.com/vacation

- Book 0 (Prequel): *Time for Me*
- Book 1: *Smile for Me* (Beach Romance in the Bahamas)
- Book 2: *Reach for Me* (Romance with Suspense in the Smoky Mountains)
- Book 3: *Wait for Me* (Romance with Suspense on a Cruise Ship)
- Book 4: *Look for Me* (Romance with Suspense in a Florida Beach Town)
- Book 5: *Pray for Me* (International Romance in the City of Atlanta)
- Book 6: *Care for Me* (Small Mountain Town Romance)
- Book 7: *Cheer for Me* (International Romance)

Read *Time for Me* (Prequel) for free:
JanThompson.com/time-free

CHRISTMAS SWEETHEARTS

Welcome to Christmastown, that holiday decorating company that is now run by Cyrus Theroux and his lovely wife, Amy Untermeyer-Theroux. Their story is first told in Wish You Joy (Savannah Sweethearts Book 10), the prequel to this Christmas Sweethearts series.

When this holiday romance series begins, Amy's Christmas Tree Farm and Christmastown have merged their daily operations at their Savannah headquarters.

~

JanThompson.com/christmastown

- Book 1: *Wish You Faith*
- Book 2: *Wish You Hope*
- Book 3: *Wish You Peace*

MIDTOWN CHRISTMAS

Big city romance, small town feel. Four Christian couples minister at Midtown Chapel in metro Atlanta, and Midtown Village, the community of tiny homes for needy families. From November to January every year, this place turns into a Christmas Village for a small-town feel right there in the metropolis of Atlanta, Georgia.

JanThompson.com/christmas

- Book 1: *Let Me Hold You* (Levi Theroux and Maggie Jacobs from *Pray for Me*)
- Book 2: *Let Me Adore You* (Erika Song

from *Look for Me* and Hiroki Yamada
from *Walk You There*)
- Book 3: *Let Me Honor You* (Forsythia
  McDevitt from *Call You Home* and
  Owen Grayson from *Find You Again*)
- Book 4: *Let Me Love You* (Leila Patel
  from *Find You Again*)

ABOUT JAN THOMPSON

USA Today bestselling author Jan Thompson writes clean and wholesome contemporary Christian romance with elements of women's fiction, Christian romantic suspense with an air of mystery, and inspirational international thrillers with threads of sweet Christian romance. Jan's books are for readers who love inspiring stories of faith, hope, and love in Jesus Christ.

Raised on a tropical island in the eastern hemisphere, Jan now lives and writes in the western hemisphere. Her international background gives her a unique multicultural and multiracial perspective to her novels and books. The island has never left her, and she reminisces about beach life in her beach romance novels.

When Jan is not busy writing small-town stories, she writes big-city romantic suspense and international technothrillers, a nod to her previous career in computer science. She weaves technology with human interests, reflecting the current and future digital world. And romance. There's always romance.

Beyond the printed page, Jan is a wife, mother, family scribe, avid reader, occasional artist, erstwhile pianist, and chief of staff to the family cat.

Find out more about Jan Thompson:
JanThompson.com

Subscribe to Jan's book news mailing list:
JanThompson.com/newsletter

*For God so loved the world
that He gave His only begotten Son,
that whoever believes in Him
should not perish
but have everlasting life.*
—John 3:16